Praise for

BULLET GAL

A new millennium pastiche of every noir motif there is – but done as a stylized, digitized, mind-bending rhapsody that'll leave you feeling like you've been slapped in the face by a French *femme fatale*.

Graphic Policy

A hard-as-nails heroine, and an assortment of strange cohorts... they're the latest to take the stage in a land Bergen calls Heropa – a hardboiled cityscape filled with souls of noir.

Crime Fiction Lover

Bullet Gal is an homage and a step forward for conventions we know and love, hitting every target it fiercely puts in its crosshairs.

Cultured Vultures

Stunningly crafted – a mesmerizing blend of noir crime caper and wry sci-fi punk that is utterly sublime.

Sci-Fi Jubilee

In *Bullet Gal* we have all the elements of pulp/noir genre we need, with a touch of dystopia.

Digital Riot

Beyond a meta-criticism of art and the creative process, Bergen has a gift for recreating the dialogue of the great writers, like Raymond Chandler and Dashiell Hammett, and passing it on to a *femme fatale*.

Flickering Myth

It's a universe that's being constructed and then simultaneously deconstructed... a revelation.
The Comics Alternative

Hardboiled, high-octane noir.
Ryan K. Lindsay, *Negative Space*

Bullet Gal

Bullet Gal

Andrez Bergen

Winchester, UK
Washington, USA

First published by Roundfire Books, 2016
Roundfire Books is an imprint of John Hunt Publishing Ltd., Laurel House, Station Approach,
Alresford, Hants, SO24 9JH, UK
office1@jhpbooks.net
www.johnhuntpublishing.com
www.roundfire-books.com

For distributor details and how to order please visit the 'Ordering' section on our website.

Text copyright: Andrez Bergen 2015
Inside frontispiece sketch: Giovanni Ballati
Originally published as a comic book by IF? Commix, 2014-15

ISBN: 978 1 78535 562 2
978 1 78535 563 9 (ebook)
Library of Congress Control Number: 2016944526

A CIP catalogue record for this book is available from the British Library.

Design: Stuart Davies

Printed and bound by CPI Group (UK) Ltd, Croydon, CR0 4YY, UK

We operate a distinctive and ethical publishing philosophy in all
areas of our business, from our global network of authors to
production and worldwide distribution.

Also by the same author:

here's to noradrenaline, serotonin, and dopamine

mitzi

1

The spiral staircase made me giddy. While it might come across a poor-man's knock-off of one Hitchcock would've deployed to better effect, I was half way up the ancient thing and felt lunch lurch in my gut. Then again, that likely had more to do with why I was here.

I took a breather on the sixth floor, pushed back some loose black fringe and gazed out a dirty window frame with a crack in the glass. Evening had settled over a looming arch of nearby Heropa Stadium.

What was I doing? Why was I here? Age old questions unlikely worth the ticket price.

Thing is, how much should one charge anyway? For admittance, I mean – if we're going to talk baseball park figures.

I slid off my pumps, dropped them to the floor. Continued on in stockings through which I could feel rough fibres of worn-out shag. A flickering overhead bulb added a certain charm to the place, in case I was missing that already.

Let's take it one step at a time. Think about remuneration later.

I stopped before a discoloured, dented door earmarked 1256. Could hear a TV blaring away the other side of the wood, sounded like that popular Western caper, *Have Gun – Will Travel*. Richard Boone's laconic voice pushed through loud and clear.

Wondered again how much admission cost. Could ask. I was sure these bods'd be receptive to queries. 'Hi, saw your light on, thought I'd drop by for tea and biscuits and check how much you're asking.' That kind of approach.

Nah. Nowhere near worth the effort. Not when a pin and gently handled flat, thin piece of plastic unlocked the bolt. Having waited a few seconds, to ensure no one noticed the B&E, I turned the knob, pushed the door forward just a fraction, and placed a pistol in each hand.

That's all right. I never pay anyhow.

A swift kick, and I found four men dressed in black hand-me-down suits and hats. They'd been busy lounging about a living room that stank of stale cigarettes, booze, fear and old pizza. The quartet gaped my way, not for long, since I let fly with both chambers as I stormed into the midst of these arseholes, selecting targets willy-nilly.

Maybe, all up, the fiasco took ten seconds max.

Carnage was worth it, another crime cartel that'd never again do anyone harm. I switched off the television, pulled up a blind, opened the window to air this place out. Studied the diorama of gore, guts, Margherita crusts, and orphaned fedoras – amidst the gentle snow of stuffing from a satin cushion I also accidentally whacked.

Figured I'd need a costume, just like the other Bops in this city. Something about a mask that (supposedly) makes people quail. A frilly dress and midnight bangs never intimidate anyone – till you shoot them, that is. No capes, though. Capes sucked.

That was precisely when I heard a noise – something crunching broken glass underfoot would make – and spotted the girl in a tattered nightgown over in corner shadows.

The wall above her was speckled in blood. Hands trussed, and a strip of gaffer across her mouth. A little redhead named Junie Mills, aged six, the latest preteen to be disappeared in this town.

I wondered if she'd freak out, but the kid was a million times more resilient than me at her age. She refused to entertain a single sob despite tears gushing down her face, stepped up, and kicked a nearby corpse.

Very carefully, I leaned over to peel off the tape, warbling sweet nothings I forget, and unbound both wrists. Straight after, I located a telephone under a splayed form, and put in a call to police. Cut the connection when the operator asked my name.

"Thank you," Junie Mills uttered in a voice her size. I looked down, smiled as I exchanged empty magazines with new ones in my guns. Wondered what I could possibly say that'd lessen the trauma she'd been through.

Knelt down and placed a hand on both tiny shoulders.

"Whatever these men did to you," I said to the girl, "None of it – *none* of it – is your fault. Do you understand?"

"Okay."

"And promise me you'll never let anyone walk all over you."

"Okay."

"Now. You hungry?"

Surprisingly, she nodded.

Detouring into a nearby kitchen, I rifled through the refrigerator's contents, shoving aside pizza containers and boxes with unfinished chow mein noodles. Fished out a bottle of Invalid Stout, poured half down my throat. Discovered, in a freezer that needed defrosting, a joyfully sealed tub of caramel ice cream. Got a spoon from a drawer, wiped down blood and gristle from the counter, and deposited both objects atop a triple layer of kitchen paper.

After I lifted the moppet to place her on a stool and stood watching her tuck in, I deduced it was prime time to make an exit.

"You going to be okay?"

Junie nodded, preoccupied as she was shoveling dessert into her mouth.

So I left. Went out the door, fetched my shoes, and proceeded up those revolving stairs to the roof.

I found a spot to stand beneath the dimness of a barrel-shaped water cooler, between some bulky object with canvas tarps thrown over to protect it from the elements, I supposed, and a rusted bicycle frame sans wheels that had already suffered from same. There was a low wall, beyond which spread the urban sprawl of Heropa from left horizon to right, and straight on to dawn. Tall nearby buildings, all art deco numbers, were lit up like stationary fireworks.

A hint of garbage penetrated the cool air, carousing with the unmistakable aroma of grilled sausages.

In your typical hardboiled narrative, we'd begin with something like: 'This city is my lover, my muse, my playground. The city, she never sleeps.'

Yada, yada.

To my mind, since we're going to throw descriptions at you, the overgrown town below is a dodgy old man likely to peer up my skirt. Call me anti-romantic, a realist, cynic, party-pooper, whatever.

2

Without realizing, I'd vagued out to abstract sounds. You could discern the rumble from the electric sign washed avenue far below – automobiles honking, approaching sirens. I then sensed someone behind me.

"Excuse me, what do you get if—?"

I swung round with one of the Star Model Bs already in my right fist, in the process flicking the nose of a rake of a man standing there. He was lucky that was the only damage.

"—Ow," said he, holding his honker.

"You should never, ever, sneak up on people like that."

"I'm beginning to get the gist," the man agreed between his fingers, and then released them to look for an open wound. There was none. "Still, how else can we get the drop on someone, or make a grand entrance?"

Incidentally, the weiners and refuse had given way to the smell of elderberries.

"Who are you, and what do you want?" I demanded, still aiming at his noggin.

"May I finish my joke?"

"Eh?"

"What do you get if you cross a gangster with a garbage man?"

"Is that a test?"

"No, a wisecrack." My stunned lack of response made him push on regardless: "Anyway, the answer is 'organized grime'. Get it? Yes?"

"Yes. Okay. Whatever."

"Lady, life doesn't need to be oh-so-grim."

"You're an idiot."

This intruder coughed or cleared his throat. I wasn't certain which, and didn't care.

He took a step back to grin, murmuring, "Since you don't appreciate good humour, kindly lower your weapon. You do know that it's all fun and games – till you take someone's eye out."

Course I didn't budge. "Give me one half-decent reason why I should."

"Remove an eye, take out my nose, or lower the weapon?"

"The last bit."

"Huh." He now passed fingers through his hair. "Well, now, don't get your knickers in a knot."

"Excuse me?"

"No stress, I mean."

"Are you for real?"

"Good lord – I hope so! There're times, however, I do wonder." The man gifted me an unwelcome shrug. "Sorry. You wanted a valid reason for objecting to the gun you have pointing at me. How about my breaking your arm, and then shoving that offensive instrument up your derrière?"

I guess I looked askance at him, but my next sentence gave lie to the gesture – even if the pistol hand didn't. "That's pretty good reason."

"Not bad, right?"

"Don't get too cocky."

Nodding to himself or his singular audience, he pushed back against a brick wall that led to the stairwell, bringing the face into better light. Unlike most men in Heropa, there wasn't a hat adorning this picture: early thirties, short-cropped blond hair, a strong nose (slightly pink), steep forehead, high cheekbones, intense eyes with laughter lines surrounding them. The combination struck me as a youngish Max von Sydow – handsome bugger, in other words.

"I won't," he said. "However, I'm here to talk."

"There's a shame."

"Depends on how you prefer to spend evenings."

"Then I'll have my arm busted another time. What d'you want?"

Cue suave arching of one eyebrow, and I already hated the guy. "Lee. Call me Lee."

"Do I have to?"

His right cheek twitched, indicating a tactfully repressed smile. "Would be nice."

"Lee, then. Same question."

"Fine." He now examined the nails of his right hand, found them surprisingly engaging. "You left a trail a mile wide," he said like he was reading a script. "Boss Barker's guards outside in the Buick. The man's bookie in the alleyway behind the block, and best gunsel 'Bugs' Jonker laid-out on a metaphoric slab – the security desk – in the lobby. Nice shooting, by the way. All dead as doornails."

"Mm-hm." My arm was beginning to ache. Holding aloft a 1.36 kg weight tended to do that, so I switched hands.

He noticed. "Are you as good with the southpaw?"

"Good enough."

"You know, you aren't exactly subtle, are you?"

It was my turn to smile. "Don't see the point."

"Blowing out other people's brains is fair enough?"

"Their hearts'll do fine. These men were low-life evil pricks that hurt genuinely good people."

Apparently tired of goggling cuticles, he squinted as he loosened his tie. "The child trafficking racket? We had eyes on them."

"You? As in police?" The pistol dipped no more than a centimetre, but came back up when he responded in the negative.

Truth being, I was getting edgy. From a long way off I caught a drift of jazz, the sirens were louder, and this individual wasted precious time.

"Look, will you let me know what you want?"

7

"Sure. How about if I told you there was another way to help people, Mitzi?"

"And you know my name. This gets better."

The man laughed, a deep baritone chuckle. "Infinitely. And I mean, helping people wise, without breaking Heropa's precious laws. Not really. Then again, we can circumnavigate statutes when need be."

This made me breathe out kind of noisily, one of those annoyed sounds that express irritation more effectively than outright telling someone. Still he looked chirpy, however, so I felt the need to tag.

"Mister – *Lee* – will you cut to the chase of what you're hawking already? Much as I enjoy waiting round for cops to show at a mass murder scene."

"Good call." Reaching beneath his coat – "Don't shoot, I'm just getting my card," he stressed – the gentleman hunted for a few seconds, humming as he did, and then removed and passed over something. It was the promised business card, alright. Embossed, with a triple-C logo. "I represent the Crime Crusaders Crew."

The card swiveled between the fingers of my right hand. "I've heard of them."

"Name's lame, I know, but otherwise we mean well."

"Bops."

"We prefer to be slagged off as Capes."

"Same diff."

It might've been my imagination, but the man appeared to momentarily bristle. He folded his arms, leaned further, gave me a quizzical look – and then tossed his head. "Hah. Not quite. Not exactly."

"You're splitting hairs?"

"Not all I split."

"And you're asking me to join." I'd deadpanned the comment, expecting horrified silence or a guffaw, but he surprised me again.

"Yeah. I am."

This forced me tooth and nail to repress laughter. "You're game. *Pfft* – when I join up, you know, I'll never wear a mantle."

"I'm serious, Mitzi."

"You're seriously something." I narrowed my eyes. "If you want to do something right, for a change, there's a little girl in room 1256 could do with moral support."

"I'm not good with kids. And what do you mean, 'for a change'?"

There was my cue for a soapbox if ever I heard one. "You Bops have your head in the clouds – so bloody busy with derring-do that you forget the ants beneath your booties. Us."

This time the man took out a hanky and brushed down his lapel, like I'd accidentally spat on it in my passion. Anyhow, flashing lights were reflecting off nearby windows, indicating that local law enforcement had finally arrived.

"Gotta go." Still, something occurred to me then. "Hey, I thought you needed a super power to be a Bop – a Cape. All I have are my dad's fake Colt .45s."

The Max von Sydow ring-in had fixed the tie again and was buttoning up his coat against a chill I didn't feel.

"Don't worry. I think you'd bring a lot more to the job description than mere guns and guts."

"Fat chance." I put the shooter away, pocketed his card, and prepared to skip out across an adjoining building.

Before I could jump, however, he hollered, "Mitzi! You'll call me?"

"Shush!" I lashed back. Never knew someone could be so exasperating inside a few minutes of acquaintance. "Maybe. Don't hold your breath – unless that's your dumb mojo."

3

After a few fitful hours I irresponsibly called sleep, I tripped out for breakfast at a diner down the road.

Over bacon, eggs served sunny side up, and several cups of a brew that tried desperately to pass for coffee, I scoured a local rag called the *Port Phillip Patriot*. The previous evening's fracas made headlines. There was a picture of little Junie Mills with a brave smile, bold copy above that announced *'Bullet Gal' Busts Trafficking Ring!* (they'd coined that silly moniker already), and a tag that this was an exclusive written by Gypsie-Ann Stellar, with Jimmy Falk.

The article went on to mention previously kidnapped girls like Jane Drake, Alicia Marble and Violette Barclay, all under ten years of age, the whereabouts of whom remained a mystery. Made me realize, with a certain amount of horror, I ought to've left one of the bastards alive for a spot of interrogation.

I closed my eyes, blew out cheeks, and sat back. Shit.

This sad exposé sat on page two.

The front of the paper was set aside for better fluff to consume over brekky. It bore a big splash image of costumed clods in fight poses; something the text explained had to do with a gold bullion heist gone south. Three of the heroes smiled out from an inset snap, bearing more ridiculous names Milkcrate Man, Major Patriot, and the Big Game Hunter.

Bops.

I pushed aside my plate and tossed the tabloid.

Heropa lived up to its name in terms of heroes, ones that flouted rules as much as me. Distrusted by police and the legal fraternity they might've been, but they made for good press.

These 'gallant' Bops, the so-called guardians of justice, were a supercilious lot that indulged in power plays – better to call them farces – with felonious peers for rights to keys to the city, along with its treasure. They didn't give a rat's arse about minor, unmasked individuals, the ones in their firing line, forgotten bystanders who were daily abused and extorted by disgruntled minor (normal) ruffians with an axe to grind.

Little people, the real story out there, sat far beneath the mission statement of these Technicolor demigods.

That was the gutter-level niche into which I shoved my derrière, if we opted for Lee's showboat foreign vocab.

I offered services (with a small fee) to the lost and the beaten.

Took the cash only to cover rent and meals. Oh, and ammunition too. Had been practicing gunplay for months on end – might not've yet been a maestro, but I knew how to pull a trigger, and left on the doormat any conscience about doing so.

After dishing up the cash for a meal better left unrated, I fled the diner. Dodged women with squared shoulders, narrow hips, and skirts that ended just below the knee, men in full-cut, double-breasted jackets, wide trousers, and hand-painted silk ties. One thing shared between both sexes?

Bloody hats.

I tried my best to fit in, to remain anonymous, dressed today in a tailored tweed suit that I purchased because it reminded me of Lauren Bacall – but I'd forgotten mandatory headwear. On top of that, developing the skills to be a gunslinger was far easier than educating my feet to deal with 1940s heels.

Out on the road, noisome vehicles cruised past. They were a combination of long, tapering pontoon front fenders, harmonica or vertical-bar grilles, gun sight hood ornaments, and tacky wooden garnish moldings.

Seriously, could I complain any further?

Having stopped before a travel agency that bore glitzy painted posters for propeller-driven carriers Latverian Airlines and Bialya Aviación, I puzzled if this might be time to do another runner. Discovered I was gnawing at my thumbnail – couldn't blame hunger, and nerves weren't something I'd discovered here yet.

From a hip pocket I took out an embossed card bearing three Cs. Spied an unoccupied phone box a few metres away.

Thought some more, for appearance's sake, and then wandered over, fetching a nickel from my purse.

I mean, someone had to keep the costumed clowns honest.

4

I arrived in Heropa a year back, when I was seventeen. Bundled up in the passenger seat of a World War Two era, canvas-covered General Motors Model CCKW lorry. In my duffel bag I brought a couple of paperbacks, a brown beret, a few bunched-up pairs of black tights, undies, socks, two bras, a black feather, and a cardigan with a hole in the elbow.

Plus twin polished-nickel 9 mm Star Model B pistols, each with a mother-of-pearl handgrip.

Was hoping I came across like five feet, ten inches of man-eating, gut-crunching terror. Something of the sort, anyway.

Had it in me to fight for truth, justice, and my fair share of strong espressos.

Met Lee a month back on that rooftop, and then shared coffee with him after I put in the call.

We made a verbal agreement.

For my part, I said I'd lay off the vigilante routine (for now) – though the wheels fell off within a week, when I got a lead on a heroin cookhouse in the port district. Debated with myself for all of a minute, decided Lee didn't need to know, and went down in the early hours before dawn.

At the warehouse in question, outside a big iron gate, lingered this bunch of roustabouts with Tommy guns. There were six. I had no idea how many would live within. I'd been doing a spot of reconnaissance from behind a stack of boxes far from street light, dark enough to poke my head up every now and then, figuring out how to handle things. Had my two pistols stuck in the back of my pants, and a switchblade in the left sock.

"There are too many."

I nearly leapt out of my hiding place. There, right behind me, someone had crept up and offered their two cents. This was becoming a frankly disturbing theme.

"Who the hell are you?" I whispered, hands already hovering over my lower back.

This snooper lifted his manly chin beneath a mask. "Major Patriot."

Yeah, this happened to be a Bop, first time I'd seen one up close and relatively personal. He looked preposterous; dressed in a tight synthetic outfit that was a kitsch mix of red, blue and yellow, with a lot of white stars. Came across like a knock-off version of Captain America, and the name didn't help.

"We have this under control, miss," he advised, gazing beyond me to the guarded depot. "Why don't you head on home now?"

Maybe it was the offhand, patronizing manner that angered me. Either that, or I was sick of mysterious, stately men getting the drop on me. Don't know for sure, but I kicked him between the legs and stormed off. At least I tried to. A few yards later, this Major Patriot character appeared right in front of me – no obvious groin pain, aside from a scowl pushing seriously pissed, and I hadn't seen him pass me by.

The Bop now demanded, "What the blazes are you doing here?"

So I ran again, this time down a strip between two large sheds, jumping some obstacles and tripping over others I couldn't see properly in the inadequate light. When I emerged on the other side, you guessed it – there sauntered Major-bloody-Patriot.

Luckily, a lazy smirk'd replaced the fury on his cowled mush.

"You're like the Flash, aren't you?" I deduced, breathless, thinking a blur of speed with lines drawn, as in the comic books.

The Bop shrugged. "Flash by name, Flash by nature."

I think I ogled. "What the fuck are you on about?"

"Nothing," he said airily. "Go home, Mitzi."

"How d'you know who I am?"

"I have a crystal ball in the Hall of Justice." The man laughed.

"Go on now. We've got this covered."

I didn't need a third warning. Having hightailed it home, I swore off solo missions.

Lee's leg of that deal I mentioned was to train me, which he'd been doing since – grooming yours truly for what, precisely, the man didn't say.

Guy was a moody type.

At times charming and funny, others an intellectual fusspot, now and then chilly and a complete wanker. On occasion respectful, if distant, the next day a self-effacing court jester who made me laugh with lousy one-liners. The swing I didn't appreciate was the self-important one, when he behaved – I don't know – sleazily?

Sometimes he smelled of that elderberry cologne, often he did not. He seemed to have a closet full of perfumes that ranged from citrus to sandalwood to nauseous.

The berries gave him that zest for life and laughs. Their absence spelled trouble.

Anyway, today I had my first real job for the Mysterion.

Hence a position lying flat on my belly on another rooftop. I baked in the midday sun, ignoring filth and dust, with right eye to a scope, a sheepskin-padded stock pressed against the right shoulder, and Lee's sublet Tokarev SVT-40 semi-automatic rifle in my mitts. Gave me the impression I was sniping in Stalingrad, if not for the warmth.

"C'mon, c'mon," I mumbled, shifting the weapon gradually, and then froze. "Ahh. *There* you are."

I'd zoomed in on a mustachioed man in a derby hat weaving through a swarm of pedestrians below. If nothing else, his Charlie Chaplin demeanor gave the game away. Easiest school assignment ever.

The expression on his face, however, was anything but jolly. Dead-fish eyes and a sullen mouth, like he'd been sucking lemons, made further checking unnecessary. The prick had

'Doctor Carver' written all over him. Just for a second, I imagined how the women felt looking into those eyes as he hurt them, before cutting their throats.

"Target in site," I said to the opened-channel radio transceiver beside me. "Sitting pretty in my crosshairs, actually. Creepy shithead." The man's eyes looked straight back, even if he was a hundred metres away. "Feel like he knows I'm perving."

The walkie-talkie gave off a few staticky clicks, but no half-decent conversation.

This made me frown. "So, do I take the shot? Hello? He'll be out of range in a sec." I cursed under my breath, kept the scope on Doc Carver, and added, "Hey, you listening?"

This was ludicrous. Couldn't my Bop minder invest in better gadgets than cast-off Soviet munitions and a dysfunctional phone?

"Oh, for God's sake," I decided, finger beginning to tighten on the trigger. "Let's shelve this stealth crap. Bite my arse, Lee."

And ciao, mate.

—Which was exactly when my instructor reared before the rifle muzzle, running interference with the target, commanding me to stop. I jerked back, in horror much as surprise – shouting something inane like "Yikes!" – since I nearly shot the duffer.

After pulling wits together, I got to my feet and glared up his way. "What the hell is wrong with you?"

He shrugged – "It's not his time," he announced – and then tacked on a frigid smile. "Not yet."

"Oh yeah, let's get obscure and cryptic." As it was past time to gun down that serial killer on the street, I began packing away our things.

"Call it what you will," he was saying. "I'm canceling this assignment for your sake, Mitzi – to demonstrate the line drawn between the decent and the damned."

That made me swing around. "Seriously? Huh. We mightn't be shooting this particular terror, but you're killing me."

The man tilted his head. "Apologies." And this was all he offered.

Shoving the rifle into a canvas bag, I got up and headed for the exit. "Well, anyway, it's too late to bump off this bastard," I threw back Lee's way without looking, "and he's off to cut up other women. Given you're a man, I'd say you don't care."

"Mitzi!" he called after me.

I stopped dead at the top of the stairs to glance over. "Oh, and pointless torture aside – when do I get my mask?"

He had his hands shoved in pockets, looking across rooftops instead of at me. "I told you. You don't get the mask till you earn it."

"I could go buy one now at Ellie Lou's Thrift Emporium."

Truth being, this was a second-hand quip. I'd tossed it at Lee the previous week, and he'd retorted with a sardonic smile that it'd be of inferior workmanship. Why I was recycling lame gags had to do with testing out a doubtful theory.

"You do that," Lee sneered. "Go steer straight along easy street."

Making my next words just as easy – "Oh, fuck you then!" – as I swiveled and stomped off down the steps, all fuming anger. I actually had to stop myself from laughing as I did so, but was pretty sure the performance held.

A few seconds later found me returned to the top of the stairs, back against the wall, playing stealthy and eavesdropping for all I was worth.

The man had remained out on the rooftop, and I heard sounds like he was kicking things.

When he began a conversation, I assumed he was either using that walkie-talkie I'd left behind, or essentially a schizophrenic.

"Lee?" he said. "Lee. She's being problematic. Pig-headed. Yes, I know you warned me, but I still don't see why we need to dally at all with this obnoxious girl. Yes, yes. No. Mmm. Perhaps we ought to convene a meeting of our brethren and—What? To make a final decision. That's right. Now, don't get all uptight. At the usual location? I'll speak to you soon. Ciao."

When the man left the building to go walking city streets, I kept tabs on him from a distance, keeping to cover where possible.

Point being, who said I trusted 'Lee' just yet?

brigit

5

On the other side of town, in one of an innocuous row of store-fronted brownstones, down two flights of stairs. The windowless basement office of Sol's Furriers, situated between a men's washroom and a storage area.

Brigit reclines on a burgundy velvet chaise longue. This love seat being positioned in the corner behind the door, an area measuring six feet by forty inches, and known to be out of bounds to all others.

When not using the sofa chair, she coated it with sprays of Chanel N°5 Elixir Sensuel, followed by a tight-fitting vinyl throw-sheet.

Once again it's there she waits and listens, often brushing aside excessive amounts of smoke. Takes out a compact for a moment to inspect eye makeup, reapplies lipstick, and is satisfied no dark roots have started to poke through the short peroxide 'do. That done, she bats away fumes, picks up a magazine, and pretends to be busy.

There are fifteen boys, aged sixteen to sixty, seated and milling about the large room, most chuffing away – think rollies, tailor-mades, stogies, one overly smelly pipe.

The plaster on the bare walls, perhaps once white, comes across a patchy rainbow that segues from arylide to bistre. A singular decoration is a black-and-white catalogue of demure models parading spotted pelts, courtesy of exclusive fashion house de Vil.

Just now, Solomon Brodsky had called order, and begins. A

young-looking man in his late thirties with salt-and-pepper brown hair, Brodsky today is clean-shaven and dressed in a smart grey suit.

"Boss Barker," he says. "Bruno Karnelli. 'Bugs' Jonker. Tony Montana. 'Lucky' Luciano. Eddie Venus. Barney Barton. 'Machine Gun' Martin. Duke Mantee."

Brodsky stalks the crowded room, hands on hips, head bowed. He also had on a charcoal stingy brim positioned at a jaunty angle, and there was a thin cigar tucked in the side of his mouth. The next words go around that impediment.

"Boys – I want answers." The man washes remarkable cinnamon eyes across the gathered audience. "Someone's been knocking over our rackets. Word is, 'tis a dame doing the knocking."

Taking a drag on his cheroot, Brodsky simmers as much as that thing now located between the fingers of his left hand.

"Point is, that's pretty damned embarrassing – I don't care who's doing the banging. Well might you say 'What's the rumpus?' but the rumpus is that we're dropping like drunk flies out there." A dramatic exhalation punctuates this remark, adding to the artificial fog. "And it's going to stop. Understand? Alright, Bob."

A flabby attendee on the other side of the office acts startled to hear his name, hacks up phlegm, and then raises a brow as he wipes sweat, mumbling, "Yeah, boss?"

This performance makes Brodsky understandably cross. He folds arms and stares. "Stop blubbering and listen in. I want you to fix this. I would like our problem solved post haste, just like Shakespeare might promise. Get it?"

She notes that the fat man, the only other non-smoker here – Bob 'The Blob' Dukes – nods quickly, too earnestly. "Got it," he claims.

Brodsky's answer, "Good," is not a convincing one.

This prompts Brigit, of course, to speak up – firstly with a clearing of her own throat to indicate she had two francs to offer. All eyes in the room peer her way, squinting through the haze.

"Can I suggest something, Sol?" she asks in a soothing singsong to calm spirits, even as she props *Vogue* on her lap.

"What?" Brodsky says, still grumpy.

Coyly tapping her lower lip with pencil in hand, Brigit has to resist snapping it. "Methinks you need a woman's touch."

The silence surrounding her marks not so much collective baited breath, but a resentment on the part of this gang-member rabble – she understood how fragile can be male pride. The only sound is that of a single overhead ceiling fan that beats the brume in languid pirouettes.

"The girl you fret about," she continues in a measured way, thinking of correct English words to express her opinion, occasionally dipping back into native lingua franca while dispensing with the hs at the beginning of vocabulary, "this *femme diabolique* who wants to mess with our bank book? I'll mess with her face."

Brodsky brightens straight away. "Darling."

An ugly individual sporting a bushy moustache, beneath a black Homburg with a single dent running down the center of its crown – Brodsky's would-be right hand man Goose Howard – tut-tuts.

She expected that.

"You thinkin' about passin' up our services for a sheila's, boss?"

To which someone else whispers – she paid scant attention whom – "No fuckin' way. Broad's a psycho."

Brodsky holds up his hands, palms out, a further call to order. "Gentlemen. Manners. And Goose, damned straight I am. Brigit will fix this."

"Well," Howard grudgingly accedes, "There goes the neighbourhood, our rep, and the Christmas bonus to boot."

There's a minor amount of laughter. "Meddling frog cow,"

intones another of the hoodlums.

Which causes Brigit to lay aside the magazine, stretch, get to her feet, and hold aloft the pencil like it was a shiv.

"Boys," she remarks, accompanied by a lazy smile, "I actually do have ears – *mon dieu*, hush your little voices now. All of us here have a job to do, in my case to protect Sol and thereby my gorgeous lifestyle."

The girl steals a glance at her elegantly attired paramour, who beams back despite the vapours between.

"Five minutes with me and this pencil will be enough to convince the bullet girl bitch that she is, how you say, full of blanks?"

mitzi

6

Somewhere.

Here.

Actually, over there. Forgive me being figurative.

I swiveled the focus ring on the binoculars, ignoring jalopies and riffraff between. A tram ran brief interference, but once it passed I was able to lean on the trellis and continue watching.

Really ought to've taken out a license as a professional peeping tom. Was all I seemed to do nowadays. Getting paid for the lurk would be a nice change.

Still, in this case there was a point. It involved the number eight. My dad's lucky digit. Jury was out as to whether it might also be mine.

In this city of Heropa, across the busy thoroughfare and down an appropriately dim, dark alley, amidst puddles from last night's rain, eight men huddled. They were in the midst of an oft-times volatile discussion. Don't want to sound self-centred, but I believed they were talking about me.

"You have got to be kidding," I muttered behind the field glasses. I'd witnessed weirder things in my time, not all of them real, but this one was pretty much out there.

The eight guys I mentioned?

All looked the same – as in identical. Right down to their damp shoelaces. With matching monikers too, apparently, from what'd I'd be able to deduce. The same name eight times over: Lee.

Even from this distance, judging by the facial expressions and

23

hand wringing going on, I spied that one of these Lees was an absolute arse, one appeared upright and virtuous, another violent, while a fourth ran interference with a smile. The remaining four mostly sat on the fence or remained mum, a stand-out looking horrified, all occasionally swapping sides like copycat pendulums.

Back where I stood, on a second floor balcony atop a grocery that played droning Greek jingles, I sighed. I know they say it's rude to stare, but this drama'd kick that warning left of centre. My kingdom for a microphone. What the hell were these mirrors yapping about?

And why did I care?

"Shit." I lowered binoculars to wipe my right eye with a sleeve, never mind the mascara. Damn it, Lee. *Lees.*

There was a trashcan nearby, so I opened it and dropped the glasses atop a pile of blackening banana peels.

Bye-bye, Lee's precious Scheffel binos.

Having cantered down the steep wooden steps and looked both ways to ensure there were no more doppelgangers running about, I proceeded along the street away from that laneway, as fast as precarious pumps would take me.

brigit

7

Three doors down from the grocer, on a flat parapet four stories above, Brigit studies that brunette. Observes every visible muscle as her prey skips down the crowded boulevard. Not exactly skipping with elegant finesse, but this was a pretty one – skinny, relatively tall, a face like some actress or chanteuse she cannot place.

Difficult to believe such a slim waif could be responsible for so much damage. Then again, a delicate carriage would never fool Brigit. In her experience, women were more formidable creatures than the brutish male thugs in Sol's employ.

Take young Bronco, for instance, further along the ledge.

A lanky nineteen-year-old with a severe buzz-cut and brain matter the size of an acorn. He had been following the girl's passage with an awkwardly aimed, oversized Bren light machine gun. "Thar she blows, boss," he growls, barely opening his mouth. "Can I bang-bang?"

Beside him, suave as ever in a slate grey three-piece suit, Solomon Brodsky leans back. "Not my call – Brigit's handling business. Darling?"

She barely registers the question, instead continuing to examine every move and gesture of the retreating figure on the sidewalk. 'Know thy enemy', the woman's late mama used to espouse, the only English she ever spoke. "I'm mulling, Sol. Give me *un moment*."

Brodsky taps the narrow brim of his hat. "Certainly."

Brigit senses Bob 'The Blob' Dukes hovering behind, even

before he commences a conspiratorial observation in her ear.

"Miss B, you think she saw us?"

The woman sighs, taking eyes off that distant enigma. "No, Robert," says she, pronouncing it in correct roe-bare fashion. "Why are you whispering? It is not like this woman can hear us."

The large man had his usual film of sweat sliding down a fretful, frightful face. "Well, we don't know that for sure – do we? Maybe she's a Bop and she can hear us talk a mile away?"

"If she *is* the Bop, with special powers, why bother using pistols?"

"Ahh, but maybe her magic's hearing things from great distances? With fisticuffs, she's got to resort to firearms."

That makes Brigit impatient. "Enough!" she commands.

A cue, perhaps, for Bronco to pipe up again. "Dame's getting long gone. Can we bump her now?"

"*Non.* Not yet."

"Shoot her now!" This mad lad had started a hop from left to right, flaunting his large gun. "Shoot her now! Shoot her now!"

"*Va te faire foutre.* Quiet, Bronco."

"*Va ta vay* what now, ma'am?"

"Nothing." Brigit wraps arms about herself. "This so-called Bullet Girl is an inquisitive one, is she not? We allow her to have these questions. We let her pry."

Acting peevish, the boy lowers his weapon. "If you say so, ma'am."

"Ma'amselle. I am not yet in the marriage." Her look flicks over to Brodsky, who's preoccupied unwrapping a new cigar. "And I do say so. We watch. For now. No shooting, Bronco. Zero bang-bang. Do you understand?"

"Alright already. I ain't retarded. 'Sides, this thing's kind of heavy. How long do I got to keep her in my sights?"

"Just put it down, would you?" She tries hard not to roll eyes. "Sol, is this game of patience to your *satisfaite*?"

Having lit his cheroot, and blissfully happy doing so despite the wind, the man dips his hat, a tiny salute. "Artistry in motion, darling. Artistry in motion."

mitzi

8

I spent the next few hours stomping the avenues of Heropa. Must've had a part-time snarl, since most people parted before me.

Thought about why I was here, what I imagined I could do in this city, how different it was from my hometown.

Remembered things I'd rather forget.

The murders of my father and best friend. The double-timing of others I had trusted.

Now Lee.

Another fucked-up betrayal? Wouldn't've surprised me.

I don't know when I noticed I paced outside my apartment block. Evening had dropped in for a visit, to find me glaring at the oddball Egyptian motifs stuck all over this building's exterior, right down to two black granite cats guarding the entrance. One reason I chose the address – at least you never forgot this place.

Scratched my chin, realized I needed to trim nails, and slowly took the six steps up to a French art deco wrought iron ingress (with matching transom). Locked as always, the security bolt was famous for its defective nature.

Sure enough, my key jammed and refused to budge.

This forced me to press a nearby bell.

"Oi!" returned an annoyed voice through the single speaker above my head. "Who's that twiddling with our right proper premises?"

Yeah, I had to smile. "Mister Macdonald? Just me – Mitzi."

"Bollocking door fucked again?"

"Seems so. It also ate my key."

"Jeez-uz. Enough to send you barking. 'Ang on, love."

After an electric current and accompanying buzz accomplished what my key hadn't, I pushed the heavy door forward. Passed through an extravagant if rundown, poorly lit entrance foyer, with domed glass roof, curved wood-lined walls, and black/white checker floor tiles. Headed straight to the single elevator, pulled across its concertina shutter, and hopped inside.

Seemed like the front entrance drama had doused the ill temper that gripped me earlier on, and I certainly wasn't thinking about Lee or his Hydra-like clones.

Hadn't been counting on a door slightly ajar when I reached my apartment. Lucky I carried at least one of my guns wherever I went, even when not on business; paranoia occasionally pays dividends.

I whipped the thing out, switched off the safety, leveled it ahead of me in both hands, and used my left foot to further ease the door in. The lights were out, it was dark, but with the curtains partially drawn and access to the balcony open wide, I saw a silhouette there framed by city lights.

Checked both sides of me, listened for other movement, heard nothing, and acted tough.

"Hold it!" I shouted, pointing the pistol at that shade on the porch. "Freeze, or whatever!"

The shadow hardly moved. "Yeah, it is pretty cold out here," it decided. "You didn't mind me letting myself in, I hope?"

"Lee. Hah." I kept the gun exactly where it was aimed. His ticker. One of eight, I supposed. Wondered if they were interchangeable. "If you're the one that busted the lock downstairs, my landlord's going to be peeved."

The man stepped across the threshold, enabling me to better see his mush. Bastard was smiling, like he had no care in the world. "You're not going to rob me, now, are you?"

"Huh?"

"The cannon, Mitzi."

"Oh." I tilted my head. Not the piece. "So how're your fellow octuplets?" Then I frowned. "That's the correct term, right? Once you get above quadruplets, I'm all confused."

This particular Lee took a sharp, quick breath. "You saw us."

"Might have."

"Together."

"You're kind of hard to miss." The deflated look on his face looked anything but menacing. "Surprise," I added in a flat tone, while I put away my gun.

Five minutes later, I got the explanation over drinks. While I'd poured he had switched on the radio, swiveled the dial, and found us big band music to mull over in the interim.

Lee cradled his cab sav on the armrest of my favourite armchair. I stood by the window with a tumbler full of straight Scotch.

"You know how Capes have special skills?" he began.

"Yeah."

"Unique strengths?"

I gazed at him in the semi-darkness. "I know."

"Well."

"Go on."

"Yeah. Right you are." Placing his glass on the table beside him, this Lee grinned again. "It's kind of funny, really. I go under the mantle of Major Patriot – with no mantle at all. Cape, I mean."

"I know what you mean." That said, I took a hefty swig. My throat burned, but at least I felt alive. "Isn't Major Patriot – Aren't you the leader of the Crime Crusaders?"

"Uh-huh. We met a few weeks back."

"I remember. And you often prance about in those embarrassing royal blue tights?"

"Well, the gauntlets are yellow."

"That makes it better then."

"And don't forget the red boots and mask."

"Or the stars. Thank heaven for minor mercies."

"Well, no one knows who I am. That means the costume is easier. To prance about in, I mean." He actually laughed, swept up his wine, and drained the contents.

I hesitated over mine. "You mentioned power."

Lee was busy topping up his flute. "So I did. You right for drinks?"

"I'll be fine," I assured, lighting a cigarette. "Don't keep me in suspense."

"Sorry." Glancing over, he held out a hand, palm to the ceiling. "You got a spare one of those?"

Yes, I had to toss him one, along with the lighter, to get some sort of explanation really flowing.

"Major Patriot." Lee exhaled an expert smoke ring. For a moment, I was jealous, till he destroyed it with a wave, saying, "All eight of us."

"That's your mojo? Duplication?"

"Duplication, multiplication, call it what you will. It's our singular skill – should I be saying singularities? – and we are eight."

"Eight's the limit?"

"Yep. Eight is enough, believe me. Your glass looks lonely."

I lifted it to peer, and nodded. "Empty as the *Mary Celeste*." Seemed about right that Billie Holiday ought to be crooning 'Strange Fruit' on the radio at that point. I went to the kitchen counter and poured more Bellows.

"I have to confess," Lee remarked, as he reacquainted his own glass with the bottle of red, "you're taking this remarkably well."

I stood over him, thinking. "I've seen some things you wouldn't believe."

That made him look up. "Try me."

"Don't change the subject. We're talking about you and your Super Eight. Who's the original? Captain earnest, the arrogant shit, mister happy-go-lucky, or the wallflowers in between?" I sipped my whisky, staring at him. Caught the hint of elders in the breeze, but needed to be sure. "Which are you?"

"Mitzi, there's no test. I can't display a tattoo which says 'I am Number 2', or whatever."

"So you're number two."

"I have no idea."

"Which one are you," I was forced to repeat.

"I'm... me."

"Tell me a joke."

"What?"

"A joke – or a riddle. Some silly pun. Anything."

The man frowned, but was up to the task. "Er – What's black and white, has a cherry on top, and two nuts inside?"

There we go. I drained my drink in one go, smacked lips, and breathed out loud. "So. Maybe you're my Lee. Arrogant Shit would squirm telling lousy one-liners, while Mister High-and-Mighty'd never stoop to such nonsense. Maybe." My head leaned back as I gazed heavenward. "God, all these maybes."

This individual here in front of me stepped up and clapped gentle hands on my shoulders. He still had a smile, but a cautious one. Made me contemplate kissing it, but I resisted.

"Don't you want to hear the rest of the joke?"

"Not in the mood."

"Still wondering who I am?"

I looked down at the floor, and then up into his eyes. "Kind of."

"Put it this way," he said. "I'm the fellow that selected you, that made first contact on the rooftop."

"You're the one that smells of elderberries."

His smile deepened. "It's Deep Midnight, by Sacrébleu."

"I don't care what the name is. It's you." I moved closer to him, placed arms around his waist, and felt the musculature there.

Didn't dream my Lee'd die thirty seconds later.

9

There was a dead kid the same age as me only two feet away. I think the fact he'd stopped breathing and half of his crew cut skull happened to be amiss was giveaway enough to his current condition.

Another man lay passing away right here in my arms.

"—I have to finish the joke...," croaked my Lee, blood bubbling round his lips.

Don't care what people say about not moving an injured person – I pulled him up into my arms, tears awry, crooning, "Shush, Lee, *shhh*. Tell me the punch line later."

"But it's a – a killer, Mitzi," he mumbled into my neck, "I swear—"

And then he was gone.

Seconds.

That was all it took.

Me, about to dive in for a kiss, just as the bedroom door opened with a tiny squeak. Two shots, from two different weapons, neither of them mine. A bullet that crashed through the window ended the life of a teenage boy who'd interrupted our fledgling tryst – yet even as it blew his brains out all over the living room wall, this intruder's gun fired, and Lee dived in the way. Saved my bloody life.

God.

Don't know when I realized a second person in this apartment had stopped breathing. "No!" I suppose I shouted this, inopportune to the last. Lee. *Lee.*

Sat huddled in a corner, head between my legs, refusing to look, as the police arrived, cordoned off the corridor, fended away bystanders, and started taking photographs. Ignored all attempted questions.

Believe I heard the bodies being carried out.

Finally got led to the lift, and thence a squad car, and delivered downtown. A kindly officer, some plainclothes with an eye patch named Kahn, sat me in an office. I studied broken Venetians that decorated a small window while Kahn brewed coffee I refused to drink, and he scribbled notes in a small notebook. Guess I answered some queries, if that was the case. Can't remember. Don't care to.

Time passed. Slowly.

Next day, after finally making some kind of statement I signed without reading, I got released into the world.

Went straight home, saw the ticker tape and glimpsed gore, so crashed at a friendly neighbour's place. I'd help Anna with an abusive husband, one who subsequently no longer lived there. Slept all day on her fold-out bed, and most of the following night too, undisturbed by two toddlers running about screaming. I refused to eat – felt ill at the sight of food – and ended up balling my eyes out the times I was actually awake.

Two uniformed police dropped by to advise my hostess about the service.

Anna sat me up, made me drink some awful vodka, stroked my hair, and rattled off the details. She had to work, or else would come – I knew that – but it was better to tackle this thing alone.

You know how they reckon time heals wounds? I'm yet to see any damned proof.

I was sick of burying people I cared about, even if I never knew I did – care, I mean – before they kicked the bucket.

The cops? They knew nothing. I saw Kahn two days later at the funeral, where he fidgeted, looked at the ground with his one good eye, and attempted to console me. Said they were still trying to identify dead kid's prints, but dental records were pointless since half his face was gone. I didn't hear the rest of the words. There was something in there about Lee himself, and who he might be, since they had trouble identifying him also. I zoned out. Kahn might've been reciting a shopping list for all I knew.

That funeral was Thursday.

I could picture my Lee making some crack about going to join the day's namesake, Thor, in Valhalla or wherever. Didn't make me feel one iota better. The only attendees were me, ol' one eye, a priest who was in a hurry, and light rain.

I had no idea who paid for the service or the plot in the turf, and didn't ask. It was a pretty enough location in the cemetery, towards the centre, in a vacant area between a ring of tall poplars.

Seven people stood distant, next to a large black sedan. They hovered under umbrellas, watching. I didn't need brains to figure out who they were.

Finally, after the end of the service and once I'd muttered my goodbyes to a hole in the ground yet to be filled, one of the seven got balls up to wander over.

I didn't care that my face was a mess. Blame the rain.

"A police car," was all this pale imitation of Lee said.

"What?"

"The joke. The answer. It's a police car."

"Joke?"

"You know. 'What's black and white, with two nuts inside and a cherry on top?'."

I lifted my eyes to this gatecrasher, took in unnecessary sunglasses beneath a fedora and one of those large black brollies. Realized I was angry beyond explanation. "How'd you know he was telling me that?"

"It was his favourite joke, and—"

"Bullshit."

"Alright." The man removed spectacles, placed them in a breast pocket, and behaved suitably remorseful. "We have your place wired. Does that make you feel any better?"

"I just want the truth."

"Mm." Peering at an unfinished grave, this individual

squirmed a little. "Still. He loved sharing the ridiculous gag."

That made me smile, ever so slightly. "*He*. You make him sound like he was somebody else. Not just another you."

The single tear on the man's right cheek surprised me. "He was."

I nodded, and then had a thought. "Care for a drink?"

"A drink?"

"Only you. Not those others."

10

This ulterior man, this dead-ringer for Lee, took me to a bar across the road from the southern cemetery gate.

It was an old, family-run establishment modeled on a British pub, a red brick building with ivy growing on the outside, named Pull the Other One.

Inside, a mild blaze burned in the centre of a comfy lounge, everything sat upholstered in fake leather, the walls were a variety of brown hues that glowed golden from the yellow lights hanging in rafters, there was a real billiard table, very few customers, and they served pints of ale alongside home-made apple cider.

Since the drizzle outside had made the temperature drop a few degrees, and likely because I felt emotionally frostbitten, I chose a small table near the fireplace.

The twin sat opposite.

Close up this way, I noticed he hadn't shaved in a couple of days. It was the Lee I knew well, and yet not. I was certain I'd met this variant before. Seemed they rotated the chore of handling me. This was the one that hung no-nonsense, more earnest – which may've accounted for why he came across older. I began to imagine him playing a serious round of chess with Death.

When the waiter scuttled over I ordered a straight Hennessey; chessman opted for chardonnay.

"My Lee preferred his red," I remarked.

"He would." The grimster checked himself. "Have. He would *have*." He unfastened his shirt collar and pulled off a moss-green tie, which he placed on the corner of the table. When the drinks arrived, his hand hovered over my cognac brandy. "Are you actually old enough to imbibe?"

Honestly, I wasn't expecting to hear the sound of my laughter again so soon. It certainly startled him.

"Imbibe?" I muttered, shaking with the giggles. "I thought the last person to use that word was P. G. Wodehouse." Still, his hand remained, so I strove for steady. "Yes, Jeeves, I am old enough. Eighteen is the drinking age in this fair city, right?"

My tumbler then slid across the linoleum with all the speed of a geriatric slowpoke, which was what I said as it did so – and still had plenty of time to witness no reaction crossing his expression.

The crackle of the fire, Vera Lynn songs piped in, the aroma of over-cooked foodstuffs like kidneys and lamb's fry – well, they were all very comforting.

"So," I said.

"Yes." Flat as a tack.

I raised my glass. "To my Lee."

Dutifully lifting his own drink, which hadn't been touched, the man compressed lips, looking me in the eye. "To your Lee. And to my brother – my friend."

11

After three brandies, I threw the mixing drinks rule out the window, switched to Bollinger, and had started smoking regularly. The music had also changed to a more up-tempo Glenn Miller selection. I was getting drunk, but not overly so.

Merely plotting a course for that bliss.

Serious Lee had started on a second glass of wine that must've hit room temperature by now. When he wasn't looking, I tipped some of my champers in his glass. He eyed the tiny collection of bubbles with suspicion.

To distract the man, I lay my empty bottle horizontal on the table. "Your shout, Jeeves."

"I wish you would stop calling me that."

"Better than Bertie."

Picking up the bottle by the neck, he examined the label – no doubt checking alcohol content, or fretting about the price of imported French champagne. "Do you always drink this much?" he added, having placed the fizz upright.

"Only when people I care about kick the bucket."

That made him turn to the menu. "Hungry?"

"What d'you think?"

"They serve a decent ploughman's lunch here – a great wedge of Cheddar cheese, some bread, pickles, and an onion. The scampi's not bad either."

I placed a hand over his. "Come on, Lee, get us another round."

He broke away in a flash, although the movement was an elegant one – at least to my increasingly bleary vision. While the bill of fare had vanished, he rubbed his hand, as if to purge it, saying, "I'm not him. You get that, right?"

I picked up my cigarette, inhaled, and breathed in the

direction of the ceiling. At least I nicely did that. Could've done the Wolf and huffed and puffed in his face. "Never said you were," I responded between teeth. "You're shorter than him, anyway."

"Not anatomically possible."

"You measured?"

"No need. Mitzi – You're stalling. We need to talk."

Having gestured to a waitress for another bottle of the same for me – this Lee'd take a month of Sundays to finish his tiny portion – I tamped out the ciggie. "What? Me, you, and the six other Lees? Or do you have more in reserve?"

"No – just with me." He had a cursed hangdog expression now, the kind that makes you want to get down off your high horse. It pissed me off in the circumstances. "The others will want answers, you're right, but they're not your responsibility. You are ours. I'll be honest, Mitzi. Your Lee picked you for recruitment – not me."

"Why?" A cork popped in the kitchen.

"He believed you had potential."

"No, why did you disagree?"

This time, the man finished off two-thirds of his glass in a matter of seconds. He broke the moment, however, by drying lips with a napkin. "I don't think you're ready. You're impulsive, a temperamental hot-head."

"Don't beat around the bush," muttered me, gratefully accepting a top-up.

Lee nodded, and stared at the table. "No point. Especially now. All of us are in a lot of pain. One of us is dead. A major part of our soul. The laughter."

Leaning over my champagne, my right elbow placed beside it and my chin in the palm of my hand, I managed a vague smile. "I know."

12

My man Jeeves had to order us a taxi.

I was smashed and melancholy enough to consider a slumber party beside my Lee's fresh crypt in the rain, which was still falling at five p.m.

This Lee pressed against me beneath his umbrella (apologizing as he did, the idiot) and he followed me onto the sizeable bench seat in the rear of a yellow Plymouth. Gave the driver my address – course he knew where I lived – and I balked.

"I don't want to go home," mumbled I, thinking of the damage there. "Don't ever want to go there again."

"Yes, sorry." He sounded it. "Didn't think. Do you have friends?"

"No one. Not especially. Can't I stay at your place?"

"Er—"

"I swear I won't be trouble. A couch'll be fine. Or the floor. I love floors."

"Right." He apologized to our cabbie and told him another location in the better part of town, while I watched twilight through a drizzle-flecked window.

"Who was the kid?" I asked at long last, without bothering to look at the fellow right beside me.

"In your flat?"

"Mmm. Police don't know. Do you people?"

"We got word there may be a gangland contract out on you," Lee said in a measured tone. "We weren't certain, and had no idea who might have organized such a thing if it did exist. I don't suppose you have a lack of enemies."

I closed my eyes a moment, fighting back everything. Once able, I said, "So they were after me. Not him."

"That's our assumption."

"Who killed him? – The boy, I mean."

"Well, once we heard that a hit might well be in the works, your Lee organized it, had the Big Game Hunter riding shotgun – or blunderbuss, in his case. But the bloke's an expert marksman with that antique. You know he took out your teenage assassin from over a kilometre distant?"

I allowed my forehead to touch cold glass. "Something to be proud of?"

"Sad about, actually."

I felt his fingers curl around my left hand, and finally glanced at him from beneath a tumbled fringe. There was nothing predatory about the man's expression. The ardour cut my heart more than if he'd been a plain old rascal.

"Mitzi," he intoned, eyes also clutching mine, "any life lost is a goddamned tragedy."

I suppose I passed out then.

brigit

13

In Solomon Brodsky's upstairs stockroom, Brigit simmered.

Not that anyone would witness that behind the impassive *façade* reflected in a wide, floor to ceiling looking glass beyond the barre she clings to with a right hand. At the moment she balanced on one *en pointe* foot to the soothing piano of Henri Gaston Giraud. His LP spins with a slight crackle on a record player in the corner of this large space.

The woman shifts into second position.

Having practiced ballet for a decade, since the age of twelve, she's learned to keep emotion in check – for a more deserving audience.

Still, *"Imbécile,"* Brigit hisses, kid-gloved left hand outstretched, palm up. "Tell me why I should not slap you out right here, and right now? See my hand? It twitches to do so."

Bob 'The Blob' Dukes cringes close by, while others of Brodsky's mob skulk behind the man's bulk. Some look like they want to bury their heads in the rack of minks and chinchillas on the other side of the room.

"Please, ma'am, don't," Dukes whines on their collective behalf.

"Ma'amselle. How many times must I say it?"

"Ma'amselle. Sorry."

"And did I not say to leave this girl be for now?" Brigit breaks from exercise to adjust her leotard, fully aware that all the men here are staring at her chest when aren't otherwise preoccupied with long legs. "Who gave the order to kill her? Now we shall have to act sooner than I wished."

"We're about ready," says a braver soul beyond Dukes, "to place a zillion caps in the bitch's arse, Miss B."

"Damn straight," declares another gruff warrior.

"Ahh, but it is far too soon for my liking it." Having assumed fifth position, Brigit goes up on toes. "I wanted her to suffer more – but *c'est la vie.*" She examines each single one of the gang members, and then flicks her head. "Boys, collect *les pistolets.*"

mitzi

14

I came to in a bed more comfortable than anything I'd ever before laid on. And at least I didn't awaken on another planet.

But when I sat up, the room was spinning and a headache battered senses. I lay back for a while, throat worse than sandpaper, wondering about this odd luxurious place and where the nearest painkillers might live.

After another hour, I crawled out onto plush white carpeting, saw an open door leading to an en suite, and hustled over there to throw up in a pristine basin.

The sight of my mush in the mirror almost triggered an encore. Black hair sticking helter skelter, remains of makeup smudged around a face deathly pale, with a couple of pink blotches and eyes so damned bloodshot I almost cried. Again.

So I stuck my head under the tap, coerced water through the scalp, and washed everything else with soap. Gargled, stuck some toothpaste on a finger, scoured teeth and tongue, gagged, spat it all out, and gargled more water.

Found a damp towel in a dirty clothes hamper and dried everything with that.

Stood there in bare feet on the natural stone floor, glaring at me. More presentable, maybe, but still a wreck. I opened the bathroom cabinet, found aspirin, and swallowed three tablets. Gnawed at my lower lip as I wandered back into the large, gorgeous bedroom that I was beginning to appreciate more.

Easy to see it was a man's, though.

Razors in the en suite, plus the orderly fashion of the bedside table, where only a cologne and a box of tissues sat, told me much. I lifted the perfume, sprayed my wrist, and sniffed. No elderberries. It was a citrus fragrance.

There sat on the bare wall one single framed copy of Marvel Comics' *Nick Fury, Agent of S.H.I.E.L.D.* #7 by artist Jim Steranko – his homage to Dalí's 'Soft Watch at the Moment of First Explosion' – beside the only other hanging, a blue-washed poster of a discreetly naked girl with a black bob, a gun in her right hand, and the words, 'It's Not You, It's Me.'

That was when I noticed I was wearing men's silk pyjamas, an ivory ensemble lacking any fancy monogram.

I left the oasis and wandered along a wide corridor with knick-knacks on antique pedestals and paintings on the wall that looked like real ones by Turner, van Gogh, and whoever else. A highlight being a framed giant photograph of a woman's eye, with glass tears, signed by Man Ray.

Atop polished floorboards sat a gorgeous Persian rug.

At the end was an open entrance to a spacious lounge. Beyond? An equally large open-plan kitchen, where one of the Lees stood cooking in a dark green tweed dressing gown. Velveteen slippers covered his feet. He glanced over and smiled.

"Which one are you?" I asked.

"Same as last night."

"From the pub?"

"From the pub."

"You carbon copies don't room together – do you?"

"God forbid."

The man flipped a pancake on the stove, stirred a saucepan containing mushrooms in what smelled like a red wine and butter sauce, and then switched off the gas that had been boiling coffee. I came closer, feeling ill, but leaned against a wall to watch this cook-off.

"Like some?" he said without looking.

"Not really."

"Sleep alright?"

"Guess. Where did you—?"

"Spare bedroom."

"Oh." I took a big breath. "I'll have a coffee, if that's okay."

"Yes, 'course. Cream?"

"Black. Strong."

"Coming right up. Take a seat, Mitzi."

I took his advice, plunking myself down on a snow-white leather couch that'd fit six people, with space between.

As I sank into it, my eyes took in more decorations: walls covered in further bona fide old masters, crossed fencing foils over a clean fireplace, a large glazed Chinese pot with peacock feathers sticking out, and a crystal chandelier above my head. Nearby rested a chessboard with only one pawn (white) and a knight (black) in play. Books such as *Brave New World*, *Madness and Civilization*, *Bushidō: The Soul of Japan*, and *Animal Farm* sat in a stylish stained cedar case. On top of this were arranged a set of ancient Japanese matchboxes.

Most prominent was a hefty red banner across from the big window. This representation bore a blue and white circle with a diagonal lightning bolt through the centre, running right to left.

Made me ask, "What *is* that?"

"That," said Lee, as he wheeled in a trolley embalmed in a white sheet, "is the flag that belonged to the British Union of Fascists in the 1930s."

On the cart sat silverware, crockery, a bowl of fruit, a pot of coffee, cream, sugar, and a plate covered with a metal lid. There was a single white lily in a white vase. The man poured and placed a mug of steaming black goodness next to me on a glass side-table.

"Thank you," I said, still eyeing that flag.

He started preparing his own cup with milk and sugar. "You're welcome."

"So. Why do you have it? The pennant, I mean. You're not a—

"

"Nazi? No, no."

"I wish you'd stop finishing my sentences."

"Sorry."

"Huh. No problem." I sipped my drink. "Great coffee, by the way."

He'd finished stirring and uncovered his meal on the trolley. "Service with a smile."

"Uh-huh. So, again...Why have that thing there, dominating an otherwise lovely room?"

"Well."

The man sat down at a distance – on the other end of the sofa.

Had the plate on his lap with an omelet atop, and coffee in his left hand, but he too gazed at the banner as he spoke.

"That was chosen by Oswald Mosley and his half-wits to represent 'action within unity', but I see it as a divisive emblem on par with the swastika. Something we must always struggle against, you see. English band Throbbing Gristle took the Mickey by using a variant as the cover of their industrial album *CD1*. And since you brought up Wodehouse yesterday, there was once a TV adaptation of the novel *Jeeves and Wooster*. In that, they used a similar insignia for the hilarious 'Black Shorts', a political group led by Roderick Spode – who was based on Mosley."

God, I had to go and ask. My head ached more. "Can I still call you Jeeves, then?"

Lee paused with the fork in his hand, pancake hanging skewered. "No."

15

Later, in the early afternoon, we went outside to an enclosed patio where potted plants of various kinds and size were arranged on shelves.

I was on my fifth coffee, had taken additional painkillers, and gotten dressed in my own clothes. Had a cigarette in hand and felt marginally better.

On the opposite side of a round iron garden table, Lee was going through a swag of documents. He wouldn't tell me what they were. "Bop stuff," he muttered.

Having inhaled smoke, I almost choked. "Did you just take the piss out of yourself?"

Head down, Lee continued scanning. "I can do that, you know."

"Well. I thought my Lee was the one with the dodgy funny-bone."

The man didn't respond. Rather than toss another 'Jeeves' his way, I put out the dregs of the ciggie, leaned back, closed eyes, and soaked up the sun.

Not that I could keep my mouth shut for long. "So there are seven of you now."

"Yep." I heard him grunt straight after.

"Who the hell is the original? – Or is he the one currently rotting in an unloved casket?"

The shuffling of paperwork stopped dead. "That's a bit harsh, Mitzi, don't you think?"

"It's true. You people won't go near his grave. Anyway, the original Lee. Who?"

"Honestly? I don't know. No one does."

I opened my eyes and sat up straight, seeing stars for a moment. After that, I turned around my empty cup on the table, thinking.

Having closed his folder, Jeeves leaned forward. "It's been that way from scratch," he said. "When we first subdivided into our eight parts, we—Well, we couldn't tell who was number one. The source material. The eight of us had been distilled equally, you see, and I'd now venture that not a single one of us is the so-called original drop."

The man momentarily drummed fingers on the table, perhaps questioning how much he should say. I looked at him, tight-lipped.

"Over time," he went on, "like children, we developed and changed in relation to one another. Possibly the seed within each—it—we— " That was the moment he shook his head, frustrated or annoyed, likely a combination of the two. "I'm not explaining it properly."

"You're doing fine."

"In my 'Jeeves Does Philosophy' manner, you mean?"

This time it was my turn to ditch the label. "Enough with Jeeves. It's not funny anymore."

That caused Lee to smile. "I'm not certain it ever was." He surveyed the empty cups. "Can I get you anything else? Tea? Coffee?"

"Cognac?"

"Sorry. The place is dry."

I remembered his choice of alcohol the day before. "So – getting back to you Lees – maybe it's like the wine? I mean, you opting for the white, whereas my Lee preferred a red? You guys having different taste as well as characters?"

Lee fiddled with the fronds of a nearby fern, tidying them. "It's the nature of personality, I suppose. Think about moods. When it comes to eating, one day you feel like chocolate ice cream, and the very next have a craving for vanilla."

"Not so fond of vanilla myself."

"But you get my gist."

"Yeah, okay."

"Good. So imagine, if you will, each Lee taking on unique personality patterns, quirks, ideas that could be equated with particular moods of the single individual." He stopped poking the plant, and glanced at me. "Especially three of us."

I nodded at the thought. "Let me guess: my funny, daggy guy, arrogant-shit Lee, and you – the oh-so-serious if occasionally droll version."

"Well, I wouldn't put things like that, but something of the sort."

"Doesn't it make you feel kooky?"

"I believe I'll live."

I stood up and walked around the patio, ducking my head occasionally to avoid dripping flora. "That leaves me," I said. "So what happens from here? Do I go back to running solo? I mean, I'm cool with that – once I find a new place to live."

Over on his chair, Lee crossed legs and leaned back. "I have a better plan."

"Which is...?"

"We do what your Lee wanted all along, and allow you to join our little team. The apprenticeship's over, and both Milkcrate Man and the Big Game Hunter agree. The Great White Hope abstained. You're therefore eligible, in spite of a single vote of dissent."

I laughed. "Bet I know who that was."

"Arrogant-shit. Yep."

"Say, you *can* lighten up."

"Mitzi, will you just bloody well accept?"

I didn't know what to do, so I shrugged. "Alright, alright." Thought a moment, then added, "By the way, I'm sorry for kicking you between the legs – you know, down at the docklands that time."

"How did you know it was me?"

"D'you really have to ask?"

"I believe I do, actually."

"Well, I realize you mean well, but sometimes you act like an over-benevolent father-knows-best. Not that my dad ever behaved in that way, but you get my drift."

He puzzled over that, and then shrugged. "Okay. Now to the other point – a place to stay. If you don't mind, I'd like to take you now and show you something. Your Lee's residence. It needs a new owner."

16

My Lee had resided in a less expensive side of town, a smaller apartment in a block called High Tower Court – even though it wasn't tall. Think a cozy place with only a kitchenette, a living room, a bath tub, and a fair-sized box in which to kip.

It wasn't overly neat, but clean.

In the bedroom, which had a faint scent of elder, he'd thumb tacked to one wall a big theatre marquee poster from the Marx Bros. film *Horse Feathers*.

No *Animal Farm* in the book collection here – instead *Cold Comfort Farm* by Stella Gibbons, inside which was a tram ticket used as a bookmark. Otherwise it was obvious my Lee liked reading comic books, most of them rustic British titles such as *Corr!!* and *The Beano*, along with original volumes of Machiko Hasegawa's *Sazae-san* manga. Stacks of them lived beneath the mantelpiece.

There was also an archaic candlestick phone on the floor, a collection of 78s by Xavier Cugat, Lena Horne and Shizuko Kasagi, and a pine wine rack half-full with cab savs, merlots, and Shiraz.

The only painting in the place? An anonymous one of First World War era biplanes dog fighting in midair. Who would have figured?

On a pin board in the kitchen were black-and-white photos of people I didn't recognize, along with a carefully clipped newspaper article from the *Port Phillip Patriot* that first coined the handle of 'Bullet Gal'.

"You think you'd like to stay here?" asked new Lee, as he poked about and looked annoyed with extracurricular resident dust on a hefty wooden radio unit.

I nodded. "It's perfect."

brigit

17

I am Brigit – and this is not the story for *mes petits garçon.*

I was born in an abandoned shack on the outskirts of Paris, to *mon papa* Louis and *ma mère* Anne-Marie, both unemployed *sans interruption.*

The two of 'em bickered like the cat and dog, until my mother pulled her kitchen knife to cut papa into little small pieces.

Bringing out the *gendarmerie* – which *ma mère* speedily won over, leading to *la deuxième* short-lived wedding between Anne-Marie and *Capitaine* Gabriel Hanaud of the 12th *arrondissement.* Uncle Gabriel 'hung' himself seven months later.

Meanwhile, Madame Guillotine – our teacher Françoise Marin – tortured all of us at school, till at age ten I cut her throat with the same blade that butchered my poor papa.

There were too few tears at Madame's funeral, and men had to be paid to carry her coffin from the chapel to the *cimetière.* Replacement teacher Mademoiselle Veronique was far more respectful of her charges.

Such was life on the poorer streets of this so-called 'Gay Paris' people do talk up. I never saw anything gay about it, unless scarlet was one of those happy colours.

Ma mère got hitched five more times, always to men with the short lifespan and much money *à la banque.* She called the process a *porte à tambour* – her revolving door.

Needless to say, I had to do away with the old dear once I came of age. Funny that she hanged herself just like Uncle Gabriel.

I convinced everyone at the service that I very much did care. Acted *contrarié*, put on the boo-hoos, oh and cried – when all I could think about was how much she had in her bank balance.

After taking out a few thousand franc and packing the bags, I took the speedy clipper plane to a brand new city: Heropa.

When I first set heel here I had no idea what to do with myself. That was the moment I chanced to meet Sol – the love of my life, *mon seul et unique véritable amour*. How? His driver rear-ended my rental auto. *Merde*, I was angry! And when I cut up this useless chauffeur's cheeks, using only a car key, Sol signed me on the spot.

Another thing I adore about the man?

He does not mock my Frenchness.

Never comments on grammar faux pas, or the manner, which is me, dropping h at the beginning of words, so when I say 'hate' it sounds like, well, 'eight'.

Sol does not dare warbling 'Le Marseillaise' within earshot of *moi*. To him I am neither the frog nor the *escargot*. There are no silly little French fries exist on the lunchtime *carte du jour*.

I've maimed others for less.

Serious.

Anyhow, Sol ran this furrier concern that was front for his real biz: *le crime*. And my life has been... Well. *La criminalité* – it is in my blood, you know?

This fine fellow was expanding both *affaires* post haste, so you can imagine the number of rivals we had to deal with – men and women both. This fur trade alone can be the catty industry.

That was my *raison d'être*. Dealing with such types. And I had the boys who partied hearty too, shooting and cutting and strangling and so on. *C'est la vie de château – pourvu que ça dure*. Live it up, as they say here.

Then she came along.

La Compétition. She's good. Honestly? *Très bien. Elle est extrêmement douée*. How you say? — Talented. Not in my league, *mais non*, but she handles herself with the flair.

Our problem being she is, what would you put it? In French we say *sans discrimination*... undiscriminate? No, indiscriminate, that is the word. Indiscriminate. Yes. Not only knocking off Sol's competition but our ally and members as well.

That we cannot abide. *Non, non, non.* It is why Sol give the order to eliminate this Bullet Gal person.

Même si je dois y laisser ma peau!

...Still, I am patient. I have other things more important, you know? I mean, any aspiring *femme fatale* has to look part of the femme as much as the fatale. It will not do to gun down this *bécasse* with the chipped nails and lipstick stuck to my teeth. And I have to steel my heart to overlook that twee Anglo-Saxon distort of *liberté, égalité, et fraternité.*

Rules are rules – or they were, till today.

Il est si stupide qu'il n'arrivait pas à comprendre.

Bronco, damn your eyes. I told you *non.* I never give to you the permission to do this thing. And you anyway screw up, end up dead with the wrong *victime* in receipt of your bullet.

Pah!

And I don't care how old fashioned or *bandes dessinées* such an exclamation may sound to you. Pah is how I feel, so pah is how you get. 'Cos now the gang are restless, angry, foolish. Precisely when danger, it happens.

I go straight to the loo. It is a safe place for me to sit and do the thinking. While my boys maybe presume I have the weak bladder, I am able here to formulate a plan.

After checking there is sufficient *papier* for purposes, I kick back. Breathe with the steadiness I discover as a school *fille* enduring repeated punishments devised by Madame Guillotine.

To further embrace *une stratègie calme*, I take out weapons from my pockets, the handbag, my left shoe, and inside *ma lingerie.* Tot up quick the inventory of old reliable: the razor, garrote, strychnine sulphate, a Beretta Model 21 Bobcat .25 ACP with hollow point *balle*, the Gauloises cigarettes *et* Zippo lighter combination – always a favourite.

Outside the toilet cubicle door I hear footsteps.

"Ma'am? You okay?"

This makes me look the *rouge*. "*Mon dieu*, how many times do I need to say it? I am not the married woman!"

"Sorry, ma'am," the voice retreats, "...*er*... ma'amselle. Just worried, is all. You been in the dunny over an hour."

That Beretta, it is in my hand in no time, pointed to the door. "What, so now I need permission to take *mon* time in *les toilettes des dames*?"

Hah. I must be getting sensitive. No need to shoot this messenger. I must go out, take the charge like a good skipper, and assemble *mes potes*. Enough of this pussy-footing around. I pack away all the pretty ornaments, pull up my pants, and steel the soul.

"*Un moment, s'il vous plaît.*"

mitzi

18

A portraiture session with photographers and artists from the press happened to be one of only two occasions I wore the complete Bullet Gal ensemble they gave me. This was for the official disclosure of my membership in the Crime Crusaders Crew.

Anyway, I recognized these threads as a fairly direct rip-off of Bulletgirl's – a character from an early 1940s Fawcett comic book.

I once did a school report on the flying heroine (real name Susan Kent), but decided to stay mum and I refused to put these people the wiser.

So we're talking a red and yellow blouse and racy yellow hot pants, bare legs, cobalt blue boots and gloves, with an uncomfortable hardtop chrome bonnet shaped like a bullet – the only diffs in the costume being Lara Croft style gun holsters strapped to both thighs (my touch), plus a mandatory domino mask in red.

Hush-hush alter egos, and all that nonsense. I ended up ditching the helmet after first use.

On the label inside the bodice (yes, there were laundry instructions), the material had been listed as a triple-weave Lycra/spandex/para-aramid synthetic fibre blend with unstable molecules, hand washing preferred.

Apparently superhero apparel had developed since Suzie took up crime fighting – aside from cleaning chores.

After I got the memo (Lee actually telegrammed me) I rolled up early to Crime Crusaders' headquarters, a lush three-story mansion at 891 Fifth Avenue, on the corner of Frick.

This was an old limestone palace, neoclassical in design, with a disused *porte-cochère* to one side. The house was set apart from Fifth Avenue by an elevated garden on that side bearing three lush magnolia trees.

I arrived dressed in civvies, of course; wasn't keen to be seen dead in the gaudy Bullet Gal get-up. That caused problems, since initially I got turned away at the entrance by a security guard-cum-valet called Edwin.

This entrance, off Frick Street, had marble-lined stone walls, the ceiling (according to a brass plaque) carved by Alicia Masters.

Once through, you were forced to head into the Rogues' Gallery: one hundred feet of weaving/ducking through a permanent ground-floor collection of stuffed penguins, a mummy's sarcophagus, one pair of big furry dice almost my height, a mannequin with a red hood, and large chess pieces including a rook, a bishop, and a knight. Next to a disconnected rectangular time machine (really; that's what the cardboard placard claimed) lived an oversized playing card bearing a court jester, in the shadow of a mechanical brontosaurus.

Peering down over the lot was a giant one cent coin with Queen Elizabeth's copper-plated zinc face.

Whence from there?

Up one marble staircase with an intricate wrought metal balustrade to CCC HQ proper. Luckily, the route was clearly marked. Their boudoir happened to be a pretentious place furnished with 18th-century French furniture and Sèvres porcelain.

Before I saw that, however, I was again intercepted.

A brusque individual dressed all in white, with a pallor and long ivory hair making him look like he'd been dusted in talcum powder, met me at the entrance. He washed unmasked eyes over my street clothes, tut-tutted, and physically hustled me to the next door along the landing.

I could've sworn his feet never touched the carpet while doing so.

"Our sitting room," he said, waving me in. "You'll need to get changed here."

"Why?"

"Étiquette, young lady. We have rules at the Crime Crusaders. Secret identities parked outside."

"Fine. Who the hell are you, anyway?"

"Me? I'm the Great White Hope – of course." With that, he pretty much slammed the door.

Brusque, like I said.

Abandoning me to a small, rottenly lit space that had all furniture covered in throw-sheets. So I opened my duffel bag, tossed the costume on the floor, and then squatted beside it.

What was I doing? Why was I here? The Bops occupied their own screwball reality far from mine. Couldn't believe my two Lees had convinced otherwise. Well, I decided, I could always leave.

Without any glee I changed clothes, put my bag behind the door, and sauntered out. That Great White Hope character had vanished, so I let myself into the main arena.

Shuffling, awed members of the press were waiting, an even dozen with nametags listing the *Patriot* and the *Observer* amongst others. Most were men in suits and hats, but one – over by the stately bay window that dominated a wall – was a woman of thirty-odd in a tweed suit number with slacks. Of all the newshounds, she seemed less enamoured.

I didn't get time to gawk further.

Knowing my new Lee, he had no intention to steal thunder, but was bent instead on signaling some kind of change to established order.

Hence, next moment, he rolled up as an additional new employee of the CCC – calling himself Sir Omphalos.

The man got the lordly title right, bedecked in a varied-grey costume that included a loathsome gunmetal coloured cape so long it looked like he was taking the piss. Seriously, the thing reached his ankles. Had *'danger!'* written all over. And you could write a novel based on the different shades of grey found here.

Taking this into account, you barely noticed his oversized belt buckle, bearing a backwards version of the lightning flag motif that belonged to the British Union of Fascists.

After he'd announced himself – having spelled out the name for reporters with pads – he looked over and introduced me as well.

"This wouldn't be," inquired the female reporter by the window, "the same kid that's been poking a torch at criminal elements in Heropa?"

"One and the same."

The woman scowled. "Capes now resort to firearms?"

Lee laughed. "Gypsie-Ann – are you forgetting the Big Game Hunter?"

"Still."

"Well, it's her particular finesse."

"And yours, 'Sir Omphalos'?"

"All in good time."

The male reporters then bombarded me with questions – while ogling uncovered legs. I had no desire to talk, and most of this stuff I wanted to avoid. Having Jeeves there was a blessing. Since I couldn't get my tongue around the 'Omphalos' bit, I deferred to him as 'O'. He ended up fielding all queries.

Finally, we got around to the pictures.

What surprised me most was the portrait artist they got in to *draw* me in my outlandish wardrobe, using a set of ink pens. I sat at a bare round table, one pistol in each hand, crossed my legs, and slouched a bit. That ought to've annoyed any hero-worshippers in the vicinity.

After that, we had a group photo taken, flashbulbs popping, along with an anatomically-bizarre caricature by a cartoonist from the *Observer*. He had a nametag reading Marty Landau, and placed me with the others before the team's stupid trophy case.

At one point Milkcrate Man made some cynical comment, followed by a burp, that made us all crack up, and that ended up being the photographic print they used.

Of course, the session was never ever going to be smooth sailing.

I sat round an improvised stage with Milkcrate Man and the Big Game Hunter, while Sir Omphalos chatted up the media, the Great White Hope was off prepping hair, and Major Patriot nowhere to be seen. When I mentioned that with six of these people it ought to be easy to find one, my Lee glanced over and subversively place a finger to his lips.

Anyway, neither Bop noticed.

The Big Game Hunter was an overly debonair gent sporting a pith helmet, beige safari suit with cravat, a monocle on his right eye, an impressive set of whiskers, and that blunderbuss I'd heard much about. He preoccupied himself checking rounds in his ammunition belt, all the while chewing at an ivory toothpick.

Milkcrate Man meanwhile removed his crate in order to canoodle dark brew in a clean-skin bottle. A tall man, he had five-day stubble, a lopsided smile, and long hair patchily dyed green. The rest of his 'costume' consisted of Doc Martens boots, ripped black jeans, and a long black hobo coat – but no mask.

For people who worshipped at the altar of covert IDs, there was a surprising lack of adequate disguise going round. "Aren't you s'posed to keep your identity under wraps?" I asked.

"A capital notion," guffawed the Big Game. He took that pick from his mouth to examine the thing. It looked worn. "Without helmet, moustache, sideburns and eye-piece – why, without even this little blighter I do like to masticate upon – I resemble any other Joe. I call it the Superman effect."

"So he blabs on about," Milkcrate said. "*Meh*, for me it's just plain easier drinking this way, and I figure you two don't care." He offered that flask my way. "Want some?"

"What is that? Wine?"

"A Bloody Mary, made the proper way. Generous dashes of Worcestershire Sauce, Tabasco, piri piri sauce, beef consommé, wasabi, lemon juice, salt and pepper, all placed into a very large highball glass, into which we pour a bottle of five-times-distilled Kazakhstani Granny Goodness vodka. Then we do the Luis Buñuel surrealist martini trick, and stick it in a freezer for two days. Partially thaw... and *va-voom*. All that's missing is the kitchen sink."

Of course I had to give it a shot. The mix nearly tore my throat out.

Milkcrate hardly commiserated. "You get used to it," he said.

"Not sure I want to." I looked around the stage, squinting under redhead spotlights, and started to sweat. "So what, exactly, are we waiting for?"

"Usual humbug," piped up the Big Game Hunter. He cracked open his blunderbuss rifle, slotted in a single cartridge, then closed it. "The GWH tartin' himself up, and once he's ready – the good Major'll bless us with his godlike presence, what?"

"Godlike?"

"Our Gentleman Jim can be a bloody wanker sometimes."

That made me laugh, but I looked down at my hot pants and frowned.

"Be honest," I said to the Hunter – Milkcrate was busy draining the contents of his bottle – "do I look moronic in this get-up?"

"I've seen worse." The man nodded at his partner with the finished drink. "You should try wearing a plastic crate on your head."

Milkcrate guffawed. "Yeah, 'cos the Boys' Own mo on the upper lip is a jolly good disguise, monkey boy."

"Enough, gentleman. You'll give our guest a bad impression." This came from behind me, and Lee in his Big O cape-and-all wandered into our midst, an obviously calming influence. The two other men shrugged and grinned.

Me? I was beginning to realize these were real people behind the glitz.

About a half hour later, once the two missing members deigned to join us, we'd posed, and the press scattered.

I was trying to find a women's loo – all too apparently up till now the CCC had been a men's club – when I heard piano sounds down a desperately long corridor.

Putting off toiletries for the moment, I wandered along.

Had recognized the tune – my mum's favourite classical piece, Beethoven's up-tempo Piano Sonata No. 14 in C-sharp minor 'Quasi una fantasia', Opus 27, No. 2... Better known to you and me as the 'Moonlight Sonata'.

In a mostly dark room, aside from candles burning in silver sticks either side of a baby grand, sat one of the other Lees in his Major Patriot costume. Judging by his face, he was consumed by passion as he lingered over the keys, eyes closed, tilting his head.

I thought about backtracking the way I'd come when he said, above the music, "Close the door, if you would."

So I did.

The man leaned back, hands running across the piano, but his eyes opened to wash over me. "So, Mitzi. Welcome to the Crime Crusaders Crew."

"Thank you."

"Settling in nicely, I see."

"Dunno. Still getting the hang of it."

"Doesn't know," the man murmured, looking down again as he played. I wasn't sure if he was affirming my feeling, or correcting my grammar.

Decided to add, "I'm sorry for your loss."

"Loss? Hmm?"

"Lee – the other night, remember?"

"Oh. Yes."

With that, he stood up, arms crossed, to stare at me. Strangely enough, the baby grand kept right on playing. A Pianola? *Huh*.

The man's gaze, behind that mask, was downright frigid. "It was your fault, you know."

I stared straight back. "Really?"

This caused him to step around the piano, walk up in his ludicrous red boots, and stand just a few inches from my face. "Still. We can move on. We can be quite flexible."

Something in his tone worried me. "Who are you? The Queen of England?"

"No. Merely one of the remaining six, hardly charmed by your gutter-level attitude."

Arrogant-shit. I'd thought as much. Placing hands on hips, I tried to see behind the sneer, while an automaton Beethoven switched to his Piano Sonata No. 31 in A-flat major, Op. 110. Said, "Are we going to have a problem?"

Major Patriot's own hands, deposited on both cheeks of my backside, suggested otherwise.

"Course not, baby, so long as you play ball."

Guns were wasted on this prick.

I never socked anyone so hard, and I'll give the costume's gauntlets this much – they seemed to have a degree of inbuilt impact resistance. Either that, or I was so angry I didn't feel it. The result being that this fraud lay flat on his back on the floor, flailing with mitts up, a streak of blood across his chin to play catch-up with the red mask.

"You ever touch me again," I said slowly, and stopped myself before the cliché rolled out. "Just don't. Get it?" After that, I pointed at the keyboard. "Oh, and learn how to play, you pretentious moron."

19

The second time I wore full-rig (minus helmet)?

In the field.

Since the Major Patriot septet was elsewhere and Sir Omphalos considered this a training mission for yours truly, the next time the Crime Crusaders were summoned into action, four of us attended.

Pompous ass the Great White Hope directed operations like a field marshal, sitting safely behind the armoured fuselage of his parked white blimp, the *Magnetic Rose*.

Our pre-mission briefing aboard ship had been, well, brief.

"Someone," announced the GWH from his pilot's chair, "is attempting to rob the underground vault of Warbucks & Erewhon Union Trust Bank, the branch over on Fawcett Avenue."

"Why?" This was Milkcrate Man, piping up from his place propped against a canvas interior.

The Great White Hope raised eyebrows. "Money, I'd say – wouldn't you?"

"Could be. Not *would* be." Resting on haunches, the Big Game Hunter polished his rifle. "This could also boil down to the illicit trade of industrial trade secrets. African ivory, even."

"Or," Milkcrate posited, finger raised, "The shoe collection that belonged to Imelda Marcos."

Which when I understood they were baiting our managerial prima donna.

"Who's involved?" I asked.

The GWH shied very far away. "I don't know."

"You're kidding? So we're flying blind."

"Look, it's hardly my fault. You men – you people – always blame me. In this era, banks did not possess effective closed-circuit cameras. Blame the technology."

I shrugged. "Then what do we do?"

Evidently, aside from grumbling, the Great White Hope liked to cite morsels from other thinkers, passing them off as his own. On this occasion, he quoted Sun Tzu.

"A wise general makes a point of foraging on the enemy."

The flat reply from Milkcrate Man, head hidden beneath his plastic crate – "Meaning?" – barely repressed his annoyance, but it was the Big Game Hunter who replied for our fearless leader.

"Ho-hum reconnoitering, dear fellow."

Which meant putting noses to the ground, turned out (in a public place, in broad daylight) in dippy costumes. Gapers gaped, police officers scowled, and I chafed. The bank was ringed by squad cars with lights flashing. The Big Game Hunter doffed his hat to the crowd, and then led Milkcrate Man and myself indoors.

A chinless assistant manager intercepted us there with a nameplate pinned to his lapel that read *Henry Holland*.

"Oh, you're here – please try not to damage anything," he gushed, like we cared.

"If we do," said Milkcrate, "you can charge the Great White Hope."

After that, he showed us to the rear of the premises, where a set of dim stairs led to the basement, and fled to safety. There were loud noises emanating from below – whoever the burglars were, they didn't care about stealth.

At the foot of these steps was a long corridor leading to the vault proper. A globe flickered above, but otherwise visibility was decent enough.

A slight partition in the wall infringed upon the entrance to the hall, and here we paused.

"Oi!" a brash voice called from down the way, "if it ain't our fav'rite whippin' boy, Silk-bait Ham!"

Milkcrate groaned. "Oh *no*. Not them."

"Bring yer boyfriend?" hollered a second set of tonsils.

"Y'know? Big Dame Hunter?"

From the other end, there erupted much chortling and the sound of high-fives. These people acted drunk.

"Who is it?" I said.

"You don't want to know."

"Try me."

"A six-pack band of loud-mouth shockers." Milkcrate shook his oversized headwear. "Mister Universe wannabes, call themselves the Mary Sues."

"Men using a girl's name. What's with that?"

"Derangement? —It's frat-boy irony, and I do use the word lightly. Relates to their conviction that young females, in fiction, winning the day is absurd. Because, you know, women are incapable of being heroes."

Likely I gaped. "Is that a real thing?"

"The belief? Apparently. Those manly dickwads down there are living proof. They have 'Girls are Spunks, Not Hunks' tattooed across their pecks. I'm not kidding."

"Huh. Can we just kill them now?"

"Sadly, we don't do that kind of thing."

"Bullshit. I saw the Big Game Hunter murder someone."

"In that case, there wasn't any choice."

"There's such a thing as mercy-killing."

"Yeah, all right, these guys are wankers – but it's also not so easy. Their mouths aren't the only things that're loud."

"Meaning?" I said.

"Well, they collectively chose the power of the Spleen. You know, from that flick *Mystery Men*? —No? Can cut the cheese in a big way, a cocktail of cytotoxic and vesicant chemical agents – with high-speed thrust."

I must've looked completely blank, so Milkcrate wiggled his buttocks.

"Projectile farts, kid."

Trying to stifle the giggles, I managed, "No way."

"Don't dare laugh," cut in Big Game Hunter, a wry smile (one impaled by the ivory toothpick) stuck to his mush. "Those vapours are corrosive as mustard gas."

"Yeah, okay. My dad's were pretty bad too. Let's get this over with."

"Uh-uh." Safari Suit held me back at the wall, and nodded his pith helmet along the passage, toward a guard I hadn't noticed before. This man, unmoving, was lying spread-eagled on his back across the floor. "One of their victims, right there."

After I squinted to better see, I almost gagged. The bare skin around the hands, wrists, ankles and face was shockingly blistered, and had an unhealthy tobacco-stained pallor.

"We shall need to move with caution," he suggested.

"Crap that," said Milkcrate. "You're beginning to sound like the GWH."

"Well, old boy, this does not mean I can't take carefully aimed pot-shots. Let me show you both a smidgeon of conjurer's magic – to spice things up, what?"

The man pointed down the hallway, and we spied with him.

"Note the bank vault itself," he whispered.

The mirrored metallic surface of the vault door – which was situated behind half a dozen muscle men built like Charles Atlas, dressed in Mexican wrestlers' outfits – offered an intriguing additional glimpse: six offensively naked backsides.

It was hard to keep looking. "*Ew.* Don't these people wear pants?"

"Not when their stinky secret weapon'd blow a hole in them." That was Milkcrate's professional appraisal.

"Keep your eyes fastened," remarked our Hunter.

I was beginning to worry that I might go blind. "Do I have to?"

"Patience."

He aimed the flared muzzle of the blunderbuss, adjusted his monocle, and after two seconds fired. Someone screamed, and in our accidental looking glass I saw one thug leaping afield, clutching his posterior.

"That gentleman looks rather bothered."

"Can I have a turn?"

While reloading, the Big Game Hunter looked at me straight. "Sport only, remember. No head-shots." He winked. "Not this time."

"Sure." I leveled the Star 9 mm in my right hand, pointing at the mirror image of a bare bum, and then pulled the trigger. The bullet hit solid steel, rebounded, and struck home. Cue a second casualty, one screaming about agony emanating from his punctured gluteus maximus.

"By Jove, you're good."

"Luck."

"Even so. I doubt he'll care to sit for some time."

Beside us, Milkcrate Man was apparently restless. He flaunted a bottle in each hand, each half-full of his Bloody Mary special, and abruptly lurched to his feet. "Enough already – it's time to party!"

"Are you mad?" demanded the Big Game Hunter. "The fumes, man!"

"Fuck the fumes!"

With that retort as the beginning of an apparent war cry, Milkcrate fled the sanctity of our alcove, stomping down the aisle with both bottles raised, hollering in muffled fashion.

Game and I ducked for cover as flatus belched, nearby papers caught aflame, and paint melted on the walls.

While that hoo-ha took dragged on, the Big Game Hunter and I indulged in co-worker small talk – all the more remarkable when you considered my last job was a breakfast waitress.

"How are you finding your commission?"

I had to frown. "Sorry?"

"Membership of our quaint ensemble."

"Oh—That. Yeah, it's okay. Can I ask – is the monocle

necessary?"

"This?" He fingered the rim of his eyepiece. "It's a trifocal lens, my dear. Allows me perfect focus on short and long-distance objects, and doubles as a night-vision enhancement doohickey."

"All right. But how does Milkcrate Man see through that crate of his?"

"Half the time, the blighter can't. He bounces off walls something chronic. Yet I suppose that does even the odds, rather."

"And do you really talk like that?"

"Like how, young lady?"

"Like that – *Tally ho, huzzah,* the whole nineteenth century British Raj thing."

He removed his toothpick and broke into a grin. "Nah, 'course not. I just happened to read all the Flashman novels by George MacDonald Fraser, been a life-long fan of Biggles and Allan Quatermain and Ace Rimmer. Right into theatre sports back at uni, y'know, so improving the toff is fun."

I stared at him. "Okay."

We left off the chitchat then, to listen instead.

After much yelling, exploding, and then brief silence, a shuffling sound approached. Game peered over the edge – and his face brightened.

"Well, smoke me a kipper and call me a trout! He did it again. Damn good form."

That was the moment Milkcrate Man dragged his Docs into my view.

Perhaps he had a partially molten crate and scorched clothes, ripped in some places, yet still he danced a little jig right there on the linoleum before us.

"*Oo-oo*, Mary Sue," sang the Cape, "I wonder by now who you are married to? *Oo-oo*, Mary Sue..."

20

I've been shot.

In the stomach. Twice. Three times in other places.

Hurts.

Figure you'd suspect that already.

"Fuck," I manage to cough out. Not dead – not yet, obviously. Soon, though.

Prob'ly deserve this.

I've done my fair share of shooting and killing. Caused other people to be sacrificed: Lee, Sarah, Dad.

Funny. Evening started innocuously before the high drama.

Was on my way home from another session at Pull the Other One – remember that pub near the cemetery? – Stewing over stuff.

The theatricals I mentioned started there.

Five minutes ago, however, I pulled another kind of theatre as I pounded cement, angry as hell, fast as my legs would take me away from the bar without breaking into a run. And, if I want to get vainglorious, I'd say they'd been waiting for me. Once I waltzed by, these patient buggers let me have it from all angles.

Guess I'm surprised only five bullets met their target.

I'd been at drinking with my other Lee, you know, the serious one. My funnier version being dead.

We were still getting to know one another, I suppose, there to work on trust issues, and as a bonus treat have a Yuletide drink. Place was crowded this time round, full of men in plaid and women in stoles, most in Christmas cheer.

Not our small table, however. Lee was morose.

To my surprise, on this occasion he guzzled the wine, and I hadn't expected what he blurted out between gulps. Maybe the prick was three sheets to the wind. Doesn't matter now.

It started something like this:

LEE: Someone stole his body.

ME: Hmm? Whose?

LEE: Your Lee's.

ME: Good golly, Jeeves, don't tell me Burke and Hare are out combing bone orchards again!

LEE: I'm serious.

That he was. The temperature dropped a few degrees as I mulled over what he'd just confessed. "Shit. *Shit*. Who? D'you know who did this?"

Earnest Lee threw up hands, and then threw down another drink.

"Not a confounded clue. Lot of footprints around the gravesite, however. Bastards didn't bother tidying up. Scum. I have a contact at police forensics working on the sole impressions."

You think that shocking? Sad to say, this wasn't the only bombshell he lobbed my way.

After several more rounds – yes, I'm talking booze, not munitions – Jeeves got stuck into the fact that my world was not real.

It's funny, the little details you remember.

On the in-house record player they'd got classy on us, were playing Claude Debussy's 'Clair de Lune'.

A drunken couple nearby competed with a poor rendition of 'Silent Night'.

I heard the clink of billiard balls, a shout of glee, laughter, and dull conversation.

"Haven't you noticed," Lee said in a voice uncommonly slurred, his eyes struggling to focus, "how some things here seem... Well, you know, not quite right? Pixelated almost, unclear and unfinished? *Wrong*? Parts entrancingly detailed, while others are rushed and amateurish, like the artist skipped out on his deadline?"

Not sure why the revelation didn't surprise me.

I placed my Bollinger on the table, staring at the bubbles that slowly drifted to its surface. They looked real enough. I also decided I now got why this Lee didn't drink. "Maybe."

The octuplet was on a roll. Doubt he even noticed I spoke.

"Yeah, it's out there to see, if you know what to look for – people resembling actors from TV or movies, or dead celebrities, names plucked out of retarded pulp novels and comic books, concepts snatched straight from thick-headed billboard advertising!"

He blew out hard, spittle included, slammed the table with a fist, and glared at me.

Without thought, I said, "You need to calm down."

"Why? It's bullshit, Mitzi. But of course you wouldn't recognize these things – they're a part of terra firma for you. Normal. For me? A sad joke."

I wouldn't say the revelation exactly surprised me, but still.

"Heropa is a digital world, kid, in case you don't get what I'm saying," the man ploughed on, back to condescending best. "A construct. Fake-and-bake, if you prefer to put it that way – a goddamned video game."

Hence my storming out, having thrown onto the table insufficient funds to cover my tab. His response being simply to gape.

You know what? I think I was more upset about tone than content. And apparently the theft of a corpse – or one eighth of one if you want to get all finicky – was a heavier burden for this guy to bear than the fact he crushed another person's entire world-order.

Jeeves really ought to've tried running the same existential line by someone who's just had their guts blown away.

Like me, now.

I stumble, fall, chin striking the pavement with a crack. Stay there, cheek pressed against the rough surface.

Pretty clear I'll be dead in a few minutes. About time. Blood's running down the slope, getting away from me, escaping. There's so much. Guessing not long. Not now. But, hey, if this place isn't bona fide – can I truly cark it? And if none of it is real, what the fuck is this pain? Why does everything tip upside down, like a dumb collage being scraped into a rubbish bin?

Funny. I have a Joy Division song stuck in my head.

'She's Lost Control'.

Something Ian Curtis croons, about confusion in her eyes saying—

ambulance officers

21

Y: What a mess.

X: You think she's had it?

Y: Looks that way. Sooner, rather than later.

X: Yeah, what a mess.

Y: Nothing much the docs'll be able to patch.

X: Still, we better haul her on in.

Y: S'pose. Good-looking dame, too.

X: Same wager?

Y: Which one?

X: How many slugs they'll fish out. I'm saying four.

Y: Put me down for three.

X: Done deal. Ready?

X: Yeah. What a nightmare.

Y: Merry-*bloody*-Christmas.

lee #3

22

He was seated at the bedside, clutching her right hand. This felt cold, hung inert.

She'd been tucked away beneath an array of drips, lines, wires and tubes. Her Louise Brooks hair was shoved away from a pale face in tangled fashion via hastily applied bobby pins. According to the receiving ER physician, a man named Nelson, they had inserted a cuffed tracheotomy tube into her airway to maintain air delivered from a ventilator to Mitzi's lungs. A monitoring box with a set of electrode leads attached to her chest acted the role of primitive heart rate monitor – all of this so 1940s.

Dressed in a blue cotton hospital gown, her left shoulder was heavily bandaged around the deltoid muscle. Beneath the light sheet, Lee knew her right leg's calf had been similarly embalmed.

Twin entry wounds in the former, one entry and exit in the latter.

There were two further rounds fished from her waist, with possible damage to internal organs.

Upon Lee's arrival at dawn, the doctor had rattled off the list like he was reading from a textbook, or by rote. Which was a possibility. He looked hardly old enough to have finished university.

"Abdominal injuries caused by gunshot wounds are mainly due to crushing of tissues and penetration into the vital organs," this man said, "followed by internal hemorrhaging. The patient lost a dangerous amount of blood even before arrival. In general, it's found that injuries to the centre of major organs such as the liver can cause more bleeding, while trauma to the right side can be more serious. I'd say we're fortunate most of the damage occurred to the left. In this kind of wound, however, the intestines and stomach may be injured, causing rupture. From what I could see during procedure this was not the case, though there remains an increased risk of infection. Wounds in the flank region, such as the two she received, are more likely to affect organs like kidneys, bladder, ureters, duodenum, pancreas, colon, rectum and major abdominal blood vessels."

Lee forced himself to interrupt the monologue. "Doctor Nelson—"

"Kent. Call me Kent."

"Kent. Were you able to remove all the bullets?"

"Yes."

"Where are they?"

"We had a visit earlier on from a Lieutenant Kahn. He requisitioned them."

When asked about a recovery, the good doctor dithered.

Looked away, glanced toward the ceiling, swept fingers through hair, and finally murmured, "It's quite possible." Straight after, however, Nelson placed a hand upon Lee's shoulder, gravely adding, "And there's always faith. Our chapel is located on the third floor."

He'd then been left alone with the unconscious patient, one who'd likely never again open her eyes.

Lee grimaced and searched around this small private room.

The nearest wall, off-white, had streaks where it had been cleaned. Most everything was made from stainless steel or ceramics. Bright colours or vivid pictures might have brightened the mood, yet he couldn't recall any hospital here or back in the real world that would give leeway to the frivolity of half-decent art.

Through an open door, reception nurses in starched white uniforms shuffled about in the ICU corridor, waiting for a new day to unfold, while others administered meds and assessed charts in the ward proper. A trolley passed by carrying bottles that clicked and clanked. Somewhere distant, a transistor radio reported a baseball game.

Most disturbing was the sound of the ventilator pump mechanism, up and down, up and down.

Lee stared again at the girl in the midst of all this, thought about the hospital vestry, and wondered: if he prayed to a god in this place, ought it be to himself and his seven counterparts, one of which died and had vanished? Or light a candle to the original Lee – whomsoever he really was?

This rang insane, he decided.

Turned attention back to the girl, uttered, "Mitzi," and broke out bawling.

brigit

23

She basks in thc tub, submerged in fragrant bubbles, and it is heavenly. Could never have imagined this simple bliss when she was young – access to flowing water, then, was coup enough.

The knock at the bathroom door interrupts this simple pleasure.

"*Oui?*"

"Mademoiselle?" calls a man's voice. One of Sol's flunkeys, those interchangeable lower types she never remembered the names of.

"*Oui?*" she repeats.

"It's done."

Brigit smiles. *Un crime presque parfait.* "Of course," she said in a loud voice, to the bounder the other side of the door, "you put the bullet in her pretty head?"

Momentary reticence gives better answer than words. She reaches her right hand outside the froth, pokes around the large pink towel there on a stool.

"Um, no – No, we didn't do that, ma'am, no," the man has started to whine, "but we did stick a couple of slugs in this broad's gut."

Fingers having encircled the grip of the Beretta inside that folded towel, Brigit points it aloft, shouts, "*Espèce d'idiot!*", and fires twice.

Is grateful there's no scream or thrashing like some other times. Those are messy, over-theatrical nuisances. All she hears is a dull thud.

Brigit's mother once told her never to trust a man undertaking a woman's business – and if in doubt, do everything oneself.

Sol, she also decides, shall have to invest in another door.

the six other lees

24

Night.

An innocuous park at the corner of Burritt and Bush, far from crowded city streets. Here, beneath eucalyptus trees, a meeting takes place.

Six men stand in an almost symmetrical circle, though with two noticeable gaps in their ranks. If there existed sufficient light to see them by, you'd find half a dozen dead-ringers for Max von Sydow at age thirty-six – exactly what director George Stevens must have seen when he cast the Swedish actor as Jesus Christ for Hollywood epic *The Greatest Story Ever Told*, minus the beard.

This circus also has an offbeat satellite: another individual, a shorter, elderly man with a shock of white hair.

#1: "Number Four, you know these meetings are confidential. Who's this you've dragged along?"

#4: "Number One, gentlemen, this is Professor Abraham Erskine."

Silence prevails.

#4: "Snakes and ladders – none of you get the inference? You don't know your Captain America lore?"

More quietude, with some fidgeting. The older party, Erskine, looks ready to bolt, says, *"Er* – Might I head back to the university now?"

That's when a hand grips his neck.

#4: "Don't you dare move a bloody muscle, Erskine."

One of the matching men laughs.

#5: "Touchy."

#4: "Shut up, Five."

Another clears his throat.

#4: "Number Two – you as well."

#2: "But – I—"

#4: "Shut the fuck up!"

Which again delivers a few seconds' silence to the fore, prior to it being broken.

#1: "So, Four, is there a point to all this, or am I missing something?"

#4: "Yes – there *is* a point."

#1: "Go on."

#4: "I will, if I get half a chance."

#5: "Who's stopping you, baby?"

#4: "Well, everyone has to first swear not to pass any word said here to Lee Number Three. You know what a noble wet-blanket he's become."

#6: "Another secret we're keeping from him?"

#1: "Some things have become… necessary. I agree with Four."

#4: "Thank you, Number One."

#5 (whispers): "Suck it up, Six."

#4: "Five – Get stuffed."

#1 (having sighed): "Calm down, all. What are we – children?"

#4: "What d'you expect? We're one eighth of an individual. Of course we're going to act retarded."

#6: "Disabled."

#4: "What?"

#6: "I think the word you're looking for is disabled."

#4: "I'll give you a fucking word I'm looking for, and—"

#1: "Enough. Both of you. We need to learn how to play together, especially now we are just six."

#2: "Number One is right."

#4: "Jeez, Two, it'd be nice if you made your own mind up for a change. But I agree."

#1: "Cheers, Two, Four. So, as with our late lamented Eight, it looks apparent that Lee Three has been compromised."

#6 (inspecting fingertips): "Maybe."

#5: "Definitely."

#1: "Alright. Are we then agreed? Nothing said to Three?"

Bookends #1, 2, 4, 5, 6 & 7 (in perfect unison): "Agreed."

Somewhere from in the distance comes the sound of a siren.

#1: "Very good. Four, pray proceed. Don't want to catch our death out here."

#4: "Sure thing." This look-alike holds aloft a small portrait photo of a brunette. "It's Mitzi."

#5: "Think we know the kid. We've all met her at various points."

#4: "Well, whatever." Gaze having lingered on the picture, the man then pockets it. "She's a bad seed."

#6: "A what?"

#4 (clicking his tongue in ugly fashion): "Influence, then. A bad influence.

#5: "Jesus H. Christ. It's Heropa, not the girl. Hell – that bitch doesn't even exist."

#1: "True, true, but these phonies are getting out of hand. This isn't what we planned for when we downloaded."

#6: "How would you know what we planned? None of us, individually, can do that."

#1: "I'd say it was fairly clear."

#6: "Really, now?"

#4: "Oh, I fucking well agree with you, One. Lucky for us, Prof Erskine here is going to help change all that – aren't you, buster?"

lee denslow

25

In the beginning, Man created Heropa.

It took longer than six days.

...No, no, wait; scratch the Old Testament hullabaloo. At the time there was indeed a guy – singular – involved, though he later became plural.

Let me explain.

This is how Heropa *really* got rolling.

Once upon a time, there was a man who loved Japan almost as much as he relished comics. He read up on everything available – a Japanophile by another name, I guess.

Of course, at that stage of affairs, the country was gone.

This man lived in Melbourne, the last city in the world. Japan? Nothing more than a memory, just like the old major U.S. comic publishers.

The man worked for a corporation called Hylax. His job? Designing, upgrading and maintaining a complicated set of virtual-reality based training programs utilized by both Victoria Police and private security firms – along with the secretive, ad hoc government enforcement agency Seeker Branch.

In his free time, aside from the fixation on Japan, we mentioned his passion for comic books. These he collected and read countless times over. His interest lay in ones sourced from the golden age of the 1940s to silver age '60s fodder.

A particular preference? Little-known champ Captain Freedom.

Quite aside, the man's favourite movies were *Breakfast at*

Tiffany's, in which Martin Balsam's character O. J. Berman was a scream, *Singin' in the Rain*, and Ingmar Bergman's *The Seventh Seal* – Lee continually confident that, if he were female, he'd be smitten with Max von Sydow.

But, as I say, he also delighted in things produced by a defunct nation that used to exist on the other side of the Pacific. Scribbling by Mishima and Kawabata, Murakami and Akutagawa. Ancient boxes of matches from another era, bearing devils or kewpie dolls. Watching films from Kurosawa, Ozu, Mizoguchi, Kon and Oshii. Collecting geisha postcards put out before World War II.

Was once in love.

This happened to be long ago. Like Japan, she was gone. Unlike Japan, he couldn't let her go.

Eventually, he nurtured an idea – downloaded every single morsel he could about Mina, all remaining fragments of the woman's soul, into an online platform he'd started to develop.

This was a secretive project no one else knew. Mooning over visual yarns and things pertaining to Japan took second fiddle.

Inspired by his comic books, he labeled the enterprise 'Heropa'. That was always meant as a temporary tag, to be replaced by something more fanciable, but for one reason or another it stuck.

All hours of day and night at home, and subversively in the office, he switched to that world, building it from the bootstraps up.

Think much use of coding languages old, new, and invented by the man himself, combined over six years. He also introduced automatic programming to enable him to write code at a higher abstraction level, along with artificial intelligence-based software development tools and mixed processor technologies whereby native code was generated for multiple environments.

A further principle element?

Graphical modeling, data mapping, conversion, and model-based code generation using custom templates he based around actors, old-time celebrities and classic cinema, especially film noir from the 1940s – along with the characters, creators, and realms of golden to silver age sequential art.

One bonus he could not resist shooing-in were ingredients from *Breakfast at Tiffany's*, yet strangely Japan barely entered the equation.

Still, when eyes hurt and fingers ached, he took time out from world building to indulge in Japanese knick-knacks alongside comic books, often scribbling post-its in relation to the latter to utilize within the structure Heropa was taking.

But then – disaster.

In the midst of construction, he lost *her* again. A systems crash at a pivotal juncture, and the spirit of Mina he'd so carefully nurtured became adrift.

At the time, our man lost the plot.

In his workplace, while coworkers ogled, he'd jumped up, smashed his keyboard, swung at a boss, and screamed. This led to a brief suspension of duties and review by management, along with a psyche evaluation. There was mention made of an anger management issue, disproportional anxiety, and a possibly repressed hostility disorder, but he put these down to exhaustion.

As for anxiety, who wouldn't get worked up in this day and age? If you placed the facts side by side, they got dispiriting.

For starters, the known world being on its knees, lashed by a downward-spiraling climate. Its survivors packed together, on edge, in an overpopulated city run by a dictatorship. Paranoia that ran amuck beneath dilating economic divides. Kith and kin beginning to betray one another. This 'sanctuary' walled-up against an exterior biological terror – the name of which no one could pronounce – that had obliterated every other place on the globe.

Scientists had dubbed it *Ex-Otolaryngology AB*, but the media and everyone else opted for Virus X.

This plague first struck twelve years back, somewhere in Asia. A decade ago ninety-seven percent of the Earth's population was dead, the wealthy remnants of the rest bargaining their way into Melbourne – the last place unaffected – and then the Wall got erected. End of international story.

Start of single-city horrors best told elsewhere.

If John Batman knew what would become of the township he founded in 1835, he'd be content they didn't continuing using his name for the place. Instead it was Lord Melbourne's fate to roll about his untended Hertfordshire grave in a depopulated England.

Anyway, back to Heropa creator Lee Denslow, who spent the enforced time away from work with his head stuck in Captain Freedom.

He started like always with the first run, from the Captain's inaugural appearance in print in May 1941, inside *Speed Comics* #13 – a product of Brookwood Publications, soon to be acquired by Harvey Comics.

Yes, the very same people who put out *Richie Rich, Casper the Friendly Ghost, Baby Huey* and *Wendy the Good Little Witch*. Certainly, they also gave us *Green Hornet*, but hush up; I'm attempting to be disparaging and witty.

Lee's hero wasn't on the cover for his debut; that honour had been reserved for someone since utterly forgotten named Shock Gibson, a.k.a. the Human Dynamo.

As it turned out, Captain Freedom was Don Wright – an American newspaper publisher during World War II who adopted his costumed identity to fight evil agents of the Axis Powers. He gained sometimes-wayward assistance from the Young Defenders, four kids who also did his deliveries.

Making them a perky posse of mostly disremembered champions.

The problem might have been that Freedom appeared hot on the heels of a similarly star-spangled officer-of-same-rank: the immensely popular Captain America, whose first issue was published a couple of months earlier, in March of '41, via Marvel predecessor Timely Comics.

This captain got placed on the cover and gave Hitler a good, walloping punch.

Patriotic (if occasionally copycat) superheroes were de rigueur during World War II, pumped out in millions of ten-cent, 60-plus page packages by sweatshop publishing houses in New York – providing not just amusement for kids back home, but urgent propaganda for the overseas GIs.

And there were *oh so many* captains: Captain Victory, Captain Midnight, Captain Fearless, Captain Courageous, and Captain Flag. Major or colonel seemed out of the question (aside from one character called Major Victory), and perhaps 'lieutenant' rung inferior, or too much mouthful.

Yet while a lot of comic people knew who conjured up Captain America – Jack Kirby and Joe Simon – and (if fastidious) you could discover the creators of nearly every other good captain, the individual behind Captain America's derivative peer Captain Freedom remained unknown.

There *is* a name, one that appeared in the credits of *Speed Comics* #13: 'Franklin Flagg'.

Problem being it's obviously a pseudonym, and there was no information about the real person behind the curtain. Golden age comic book aficionados relegated truth in the matter to the waste paper bins of history.

Much like the rest of the world, really.

Yet while a moniker (even a fake one) like Franklin Flagg comes across stalwart and punchy, Captain Freedom, it would seem, had lacked similar self-assured conviction.

During a six-year period in which Captain America only swapped shields and slightly amended his mask, Don Wright undertook a swathe of wardrobe design alterations.

When first he appeared (on page 61 of the aforementioned

Speed Comics #13), our hero wore a red skullcap without mask, he had a circle of stars on the chest, and Captain America's red-and-white stripes on the waistline of his blue tunic. He also had yellow shoulder pads, bore no sleeves or gloves, boasted blue hot pants without trouser-legs, and simple brown boots.

Four issues later, in 1942, Freedom had adopted a V-shaped star formation on his chest, red gauntlets, and a cowl that covered the top of his face, with a star on the forehead – making him more Captain America than ever.

By #19, he'd lost the peck-stripes; the gloves were yellow, while the star was on top of his head.

If you downloaded into Heropa proper, and you *really* knew golden era superhero mythos, you'd recognize the suit(s) worn by Major Patriot were a hybrid of the Captain Patriot costumes from #17 and 19.

When the final edition of *Speed Comics* (#44) was published in 1947, the man had again lost his pants.

Still, much as we might mock Donald Wright as a poor-man's Steve Rogers, it looks like he ended up on the drafting table of Rogers' creators Simon and Kirby.

There is a persuasive argument that this duo worked under the epithet of 'Jon Henri' – the name on the cover for *Speed Comics* #17 (April, 1942). It's further contended Joe Simon did the Captain Freedom artwork inside (along with other issues) and that Simon, again with Jack Kirby, composed the striking cover for #22.

While Captain America went on ice for a couple of decades – at least in the reinvented Marvel Comics scheme of things when Kirby and Stan Lee brought the character back in March, 1964 in the pages of *The Avengers* – Captain Freedom sank without trace after *Speed* was cancelled in 1947.

Which brings us to our hero's second incarnation, another series Lee collected and read back to back after the first.

In the 1980s, the character got rebooted, with different powers and a gaudy new costume, by Americomics (later AC Comics). This time round Captain Freedom was a batch of clones made from the DNA of a deceased famous scientist, located all over the world to provide each nation with its own protector. He had his own series as well as a spin-off titled *Soldiers of Freedom*.

Ahh, Captain Freedom. Lee never got tired of the disjointed journey.

After closing the covers of *Men of Mystery* #89 – a 240-page AC reprinting (in 2013) of obscure golden age superhero stories including Freedom and even Shock Gibson, Lee stretches legs and rises from the couch.

Heads to the window of his tiny apartment, opens the blind, and peers out at a dirty downpour that attempted, in its way, to tarnish a city already filthy.

Melbourne. Shit.

He thinks instead again about Cap Freedom, of what he would have done with the character if he were creator, writer, artist, or a combination of all three. So much potential there.

Sometimes it saddened Lee that people were more likely to recall an unrelated Captain Freedom character played by actor/wrestler Jesse Ventura in the 1987 Arnold Schwarzenegger flick *The Running Man*.

Mina.

He softly bangs his head against warm, moist glass. The real thing he was running from, burying his head in comics. How was he going to rediscover Mina?

In the condensation on the window, with an index finger, he draws a series of stick figures. There were eight once he finished, all reasonably similar, each with a mask and overlarge stars. On the middle character he added a halo, while the one on the left had a giant penis, just to make them different, but upon second thought he struck out the willy since that was too much.

And then – the idea struck him back.

Lee staggered from the window ledge. His mouth wide open,

he stares at those crude drawings at attention between him and the depths of depravity that Melbourne had become.

Heropa.

Why not go into the system to *find* her?

Pacing the carpet, weaving through piles of comics carefully wrapped in Mylar four-millimetre sleeves, Lee tries to think quickly and clearly. No one need know. He could do this in free time, and in fact had earned weeks of annual leave without taking a single day till now. The 'breakdown' at work offered good excuse to take an overdue vacation.

Why not go into the system *and find her*?

He stops, laughs – and then shakes his head.

Not so fast. The problem here being his own creation: Heropa was one massive slab of digital terrain to investigate alone. Who needed a haystack?

Rubbing his chin, pondering this issue, Lee glances at the 'zines by his feet.

What would Captain Freedom do? How would Don Wright handle this? Well, he'd require help. Freedom wasn't above working with the Young Defenders.

So, one way to circumvent the problem would be to open his existing Heropa platform to others – covertly, of course.

Surely certain people would delight in a form of reverential soma holiday.

Lee's gaze settles on the cover of #1 of the rebooted *Captain Freedom* comic from 1983, which had the subtitled caption-in-a-box, 'To Steal the Sun'. Depicting our hero swinging away from a golden, fiery orb, it reminds him of the clones.

Of course.

Since the very purview of Heropa was to grant players a unique skill or 'super power', just like in comics – Well, why not go with the latter-day Captain's mojo and therefore have more feet on the ground?

To find her, somehow. His Mina.

The thought makes him reel. It hurt still to remember. He pushes palms into his eyes, trying to stop seeing the flow of memories. Yet why could he no longer clearly view her face?

So, Lee resolves, dropping hands as he banishes a recollected kiss – enough with the stalling and self-pity. There were things that now needed to be done in order to get the stratagem in motion.

Of course, he had to finish building the site.

On the sly, outside of chores for Management Control Division and the other contractors. There were still minor details to get just right, including likenesses and names filched from that back-catalogue cultural cache he preferred, and which we already discussed.

The hoi polloi of Heropa, Lee decided, could fend for their digital selves. With some automated AI-based programs in place, they'd develop as the world took root.

Architecturally, the platform had assumed a 1940s flavour, nodding to the swinging '60s along with the sharp Art Deco lines and Soviet Formalism of the 1920s.

Wardrobes had been filched from the Bogie/Bacall version of *The Big Sleep* as much as *Singin' in the Rain*, other attire based on the silver screen cut-and-weave of costume designers Edith Head, Eiko Ishioka, Irene Lentz, Jean Louis, and Walter Plunkett. He even additionally injected Clark Gable's personal dressing gown, one used while the great man was off-screen during filming for *Gone with the Wind*.

Along the thoroughfares drove flash vintage vehicles – most reeking the elegance, glamour, and retro-modernity (if impracticality) of the Deco putsch beginning in the 1930s. Picture cars like your Delahayes and Talbot-Lagos, or a rare-as-hen's-teeth Phantom Corsair – but Lee also allowed in next generation numbers, such as Steve McQueen's iconic Jaguar D-Type.

Still, functional traffic like trucks and cabs and Greyhound buses were important. To these he added the 1920s W6-class tram from Melbourne's distant past, a replica of New York's mid twentieth century elevated railroad design, and tossed up bonus Zeppelin-style airship networks that plied for passage above the soaring skyline.

Erected statuary that paid homage to the pioneering lions of sequential art such as Wood, Eisner, Steranko, Hergé, Tezuka, Ditko, Kubert, Kirby, Infantino, Adams, and Pitt; named streets after comic book publishing companies or ones appropriated from the literature of Dashiell Hammett and Raymond Chandler.

Chandler's short stories 'Goldfish', 'Finger Man' and 'Killer in the Rain' figured lightly; also in the mix were several different Sherlock Holmes tales by Arthur Conan Doyle, *Erewhon: or, Over the Range* by Samuel Butler, Hammett's *Red Harvest* playing minor fiddle, H.G. Wells' *War of the Worlds*, and E. H. Gombrich's *The Story of Art*.

Details, details.

Plumbing and a sewerage system were ripped from Georges-Eugène Haussmann's nineteenth century blueprints (updated by C. Auguste Dupin) for renovation of the water works of Paris. These might have been outdated and hardly suitable for such a large city based on a model a hundred years later – but what the hell, it seemed to function.

On a whim, he decided to abolish an ability to fly from the superhuman traits available.

None of his favourite comic book characters needed to do this – not Captains Freedom or America, Batman, Spider-Man, Green Arrow, Daredevil, the Black Canary, Hawkeye, Magpie, the Thing, whoever.

Sure, they used technology occasionally to cheat this, but the native skill of flight would be erased. No Superman here. And while on the subject of the Man of Steel, he also banned invulnerability.

Heropa City's official flag?

A navy blue number with a sailing ship dead centre, inside a yellow rope and two crossed swords behind, with several golden stars around that – a riff on the Gotham flag from Christopher Nolan's Batman film *Dark Knight*.

Shops, stores, theatres, bank and hotels shared names with those found in the early issues of *Fantastic Four* and *Tales to Astonish*, or in *Batman* and *Little Orphan Annie*.

Hating creepy-crawlies, Lee decided early to dispense with most of these – aside from bees (useful with flora and honey), ants (always good workers), and cicadas (for the sounds of summer he missed from childhood).

Going in deeper, electromagnetic radiation – with wavelengths in the electromagnetic spectrum longer than infrared light – needed to be applied, in order to provide radio waves on which Heropa's broadcasters could function.

Adding some self-satisfied amusement?

Sliding in silly nods and references, mostly to movies and comics, but also to his hometown – hence incorporating a major Melbourne newspaper (the *Port Phillip Patriot*) that in reality ceased publication in 1851.

The Heropa *Patriot*'s offices had been modelled on the Marine Building, an Art Deco skyscraper in Vancouver that – at 98 metres – had been the tallest building in the world from 1930-39.

This Marine Building was used to fill in as *Daily Planet* headquarters in TV show *Smallville* (Lee's Heropa version utilizing the same address: 335/1000 Broadway), and it stood in for the Baxter Building in 2005's *Fantastic Four* movie.

So, yep, the place was perfect to carbon copy.

Dishing up some hilarious Escher stairwells around the digital city itself – to confuse the unsuspecting – was an aside. After finishing all that, Lee could take a hard-earned vacation... and go find his girl.

Our boy glances again at the window.

Yes, he decides.

Eight ought to do it.

bob

26

In a rubble-filled arch beneath the H-Train railway, standing alone, he stared up at shoddy graffiti on the brickwork that depicted a smiley face with an eyepatch.

Beneath that portrait were painted the words *Ol' one eye sucks!* and zero else. No autograph to go by. Still, the curvature of this script, which tilted to the left, gave him an idea who the slipshod artist might be.

He'd need to have another stern chat with Red Hargrove's folks.

"Bloody hell," he muttered.

He hadn't intended this gripe about graf he was pretty sure meant to portray him – not many other fellows in this city had a patch covering their left peeper, let alone ones that'd inspire this kind of lame-arse pisstake.

No, he was talking up Heropa. His city. His beat.

Swiveling on a heel in loose gravel, the man looked both ways down an empty street that was beginning to lose shadows in the pre-dawn hue.

He had no intention of wasting time to serenade praises about a town that never sleeps (everyone here appeared to be tucked in), or draw parallels with a concrete lady that broke your heart on a daily basis. Natch both. Thing being, Heropa could prove either – if you let it take hold. A safer alternative was to glide beneath the radar, make few waves aside from the occasional arrest (the press and the commissioner loved those), and do everything by the book.

In his case? The *Police Dept. Rules and Regulations and Manual of Procedure of Police Department of the City of Heropa* (2nd Edition).

Walking forward with hands in pockets, his mustard-yellow trench coat swirled in a light breeze that carried with it the odours of fuel and dung.

Thirty-one year old police detective Robert Joseph 'Bob' Kahn, the eldest of three children born to Jack Kahn and Nia Jones, liked to keep things simple.

He hated it when people got sentimental about their hometown. It remained just a city, for crap's sake. But talking about *people* – they were what mattered. The ones he tried to focus upon.

In a hospital just south of here, a young girl lay dying.

Ambushed by half a dozen cheap hoodlums, while police officers stood idly by – men he'd assigned to watch out for this kid, after her friend was murdered in an undoubted gangland slaying. The two constables made a rousing song and dance about being unable to intervene in time, for their allowing vicious gunmen to escape into the night.

Kickbacks have that effect.

One rule he learned on the job – keep your balls safe but always play on the right side of the law. Never, ever, tip your mitt in the till.

Another thing: With only one working eye, you can afford fifty percent of the trust other cops take for granted.

Stick to what you knew. Train, practice, hone skills. You were a goddamned detective, so go out there and act like one.

The decaying red-brick Victorian warehouse, ahead, sat slyly quiet. No one to be seen keeping guard, but he never took that for granted. Kahn stopped, scrutinized every window this side of the premises. Some were boarded-up, others sporting broken glass or torn fly wire.

Much of the time, the police cleaned up messes the Capes had no time for. Figured he wouldn't bother either, if he could leap relatively tall buildings in a single bound.

So – stay true to the letter of the law.

Simple.

He reached beneath the coat, undid the leather holster there, and drew a .38 Model 10. It happened to be his job to bring butchers to justice – and, right now, this was the only way he knew how.

Crossing a wide space of uneven asphalt, cracked in places with weeds growing through gaps, the man approached a side entrance that was chained and padlocked. Briefly considered the multitude of risks, and then ignored the lot.

Having jimmied the lock, he ventured inside. Passed overturned clothes racks covered in dust and grime, noting footprints around them. Dripping water sounded close by. He stopped to listen for more. Nothing came, so he marked time.

There.

A hushed conversation, further on into the storage place, where stygian depths kindly offered a warm welcome.

Kahn took to a wall, keeping close by feeling its rough, dirty surface, and edged along toward those voices.

From a doorway further along, the murmur was joined by a diffused, appreciated light source that flickered. Candles, he assumed. No electricity here.

Clutched in both hands, he held up his pistol. *Steady now*, the man commanded. *By the book. Nice and simple.*

He chose the very next moment to launch himself into the glow.

"Police!" Kahn barked. "Hands in the air!"

The combined reaction of the people in this small, windowless room was exactly as he expected – panicked. One or two jumped, but the rest grabbed at firearms, and the dull glint of steel became his cue to start shooting.

Returning gunfire was minimal and fortuitously ineffective, aside from some woodchips he needed to brush away from his lapel.

The body-count ended up numbering five. *They're the enemy,* he reminded himself. Didn't make any of this easier.

27

The brand new, run down crime scene had been secured, an Evidence Collection Team made a showing, photographs were taken, bodies carted off to the morgue, and a ridiculous amount of paperwork filed. All of that took seven hours.

After, following a hastily scoffed down lunch, Kahn attended a parley. Something hardly by the book – an irregular, off-the-cuff thing.

Sir Omphalos met him in a parking lot close by Heropa General Hospital. The Cape remained in shadows, out of the afternoon sun or sight by passersby. His costume's dark colours assisted this deception.

"How did it go?" the man inquired.

Kahn raised shoulders. "It went."

That caused the Cape's mouth to briefly take a hard, straight line. "I meant, how did you go with the felons."

"I know what you're on about, Sir Omphalos," Kahn said. "I'm half-blind, not half-deaf." He breathed out before continuing. "But, yeah, I did locate the bastards. There were five of them, holed-up in a warehouse, actually just a couple of miles from here."

"And?"

"I dropped by to say hello."

"Did you at least leave someone alive, detective?"

"Sadly? These individuals preferred to speak with their muzzles rather than their mouths. But I got you a lead anyway."

Kahn handed over the photo he'd been carrying, placing it onto the palm of an outstretched grey gauntlet.

"Brigit: last-name-unknown, age unknown, current address a mystery. Fingered by an associate of mine – he reckons she's principle assassin for a crook named Solomon Brodsky. Ring any bells?"

The Cape answered straight off. "None."

"Well, he's on the rise in this city, a man to be concerned about. Hides behind the legitimacy of a fur trade franchise. Word on the street is that this Brigit character is the real brains behind Brodsky, as much as his best trigger. Don't go thinking this shiela is a plain old femme fatale – the girl is a full-blown *femme diabolique*, if you excuse my Dutch. I'm ninety-odd percent sure she's the one that orchestrated the hit on your friend."

"Ah."

"*Ah*? You don't sound overly concerned."

"Sorry." The 'O' on this man's mask sagged a fraction upon his forehead. "To the contrary, Bob. I am – and grateful for your help."

Crossing arms across his chest, Kahn tried to see more detail beyond the cowl running interference. There sat something familiar about this guy with his Nordic facial features and penetrating blue eyes. "Whatever. I didn't really do it for you."

"No?"

"The kid deserved someone making this wrong right."

"*Deserves*. Mitzi's still with us."

"Good to hear. Will she—?"

"I don't know."

Next, it was the masked man's turn to offer a gift: a beige manila folder, tied with pink yarn.

"What's this?" asked Kahn, fingering it suspiciously.

"Favour for a favour."

"I already owed you for saving my neck. Prefer not to be in further debt."

Sir Omphalos perhaps unconsciously passed that gloved hand over his left shoulder, the one that just last week had taken a bullet intended for the police officer. "Then see it as something that needs to be tackled by the right people before it's taken too far."

"You think I'm 'right people'?"

"I do."

"You're game."

"I need to start trusting others."

"Sounds serious."

The Big O nodded. "It could be."

"All right. Do I need to thank you?"

"Examine the contents first."

28

As he trudged toward a car parked on the other side of the lot, that folder tucked under his right arm and hands shoved into the pockets of his coat, Bob Kahn had one principle thought: *Well, that's done.*

Then he had to deal with his junior partner.

Officer Irving Forbush, aged thirty-three, was a redhead two inches shorter than Kahn and significantly more portly. He stood in a carelessly-fitted suit beside the black Plymouth, leaning on its roof, fedora barely coping on the rear of his skull.

"Anyhoo, boss, you're all finished here?" this man said in a testy manner, one that belied his usual easy drawl.

"For now."

"What's with the dang belated Christmas present?"

Kahn had forgotten about the dossier, tugged at his ear. "I don't know."

"So one more Bop to add to the list of caped clowns?"

"Steady, Irv." The detective fished out keys and climbed inside.

Seconds later, Forbush settled in beside him.

"Well," the passenger said, "at least this customer dresses down, 'side from the fancy mantle. That Major Patriot joker? Bloke's got enough stars to rent himself out as a walk of fame."

Kahn turned the key in the ignition, muttered, "Agreed," and allowed the engine to idle for a while. He had binoculars in the glove compartment, which he flicked open, grasping them to start checking the surrounding area. "And nothing stops us from keeping an eye out."

"Yup. Hey, you ever thought of investing in a pair of monoculars, boss?"

"Then they wouldn't be a pair." There was no sign of any Cape to be found. The beknighted gent had vanished. "Do monoculars actually exist?"

Forbush had lit up a cigarette and blew out the match. He then flicked it through the open window. "There's an opening to make you rich and famous."

Sighing, the other man placed field-glasses on his lap, pondered some more, and released the brake.

"Doubt there're enough one-eyed Peeping Toms to make the investment worthwhile," he said.

lee #3

29

He regrets everything.

His brand of stupidity, most of all.

Telling Mitzi the truth about Heropa, apportioning it on a platter like some kind of trite decoration. Turning her world upside down – destroying it, actually.

And the report had come back this morning from Forensic Services. A courier in a neat blue uniform, the same colour as Mitzi's hospital wardrobe, requesting a signature and expecting a tip.

It took the scientists four weeks to confirm what he already suspected: that the sole-impressions in mud surrounding Lee Number Eight's grave belonged to a set of shoes he had in the entrance. Eight identical pairs of sneakers he'd acquired with all other seven Lees from a bargain sale at Grace Brothers.

The analysts had been confused, though. They'd found numbers imprinted along with the prints, found a legible '2', '4', '6' and '7'.

That had been Number Two's touch. He carved eight pairs of numbers into the rubber soles. Might've been unable to disagree with a single person, but he loved his handicrafts, and figured it might prevent friction if each Lee knew which footwear belonged to whom.

At the kitchen table, seated by an airy bay window, he has documents spread out before him. These include medical reports and bills, as well as copies of police investigation missives from both the murder of Mitzi's Lee and the attack on her – less than five hundred metres from Pull the Other One.

He toys with his lower lip, thinking of that particular night. How he'd been unconscionably stressed and taken to his cups, drinking far too much, lost focus, and made the big reveal.

Having closed eyes a moment, Lee reopens them, picks up the Admissions Report from Heropa General Hospital, reads, and thereafter groans. Five bullet wounds, massive loss of blood, prognosis desperately poor. He could see from the medicos' notes they expected her to expire before a new day began.

Nearly four weeks later she still clung to life, baffling experts.

For at least the hundredth time, his mind goes back to their Christmas drinks.

Why had he not heard the gunfire only half a kilometre away? How was that possible?

Too busy drowning sorrows, likely. Preoccupied with himself and his dilemmas, selfish, self-centred, behaving like this girl didn't matter.

From outside the open window, Lee hears mockingbirds singing in the branches of an elm quite close by, erasing the sounds of traffic. He inhales air, notes fragrances of coffee, toasted bread, and a new floral dishwashing liquid he was trying out.

Touching the table top, he runs fingers across the smooth surface. Looks around to take in the multitude of subtle colours in this kitchen alone, and the warmth of sunlight filtering through glass. He observes dust molecules swirling within its rays.

Understands that none of this is real.

When he peers inward, to try to remember Melbourne, let alone its warts, the place comes across like a vaguely familiar fantasy – perhaps even one eighth of one.

How can this, any of this, be more palpable than home?

bob

30

The dossier that Sir Omphalos had provided Kahn with proved to be more than merely enlightening.

He sat sifting through the contents over several hours and more cups than that of strong black coffee.

It included the minutes of a City Council meeting, attached to several rough sketches of a Medusa's head on a shield. Added in were additional pages of stats, photographs of various Capes – heroes as well as blackguards – and a joint proposal.

There was a lot of legal jargon the police officer could not get his head around, but the gist rang through loud and clear.

Mayor Bob Brown with Attorney-General Brian O'Brien had together floated the idea of an inter-agency organization to combat espionage, law enforcement, and counter-terrorism, while simultaneously serving as the city's prime arm of the law.

It would be an apparatus that reported to both the Mayoral and Attorney-General's Offices.

They called this repackaging and reallocation of law enforcement assets the *Alliance of Extant Governments' Intracity Security*, or more simply AEGIS.

AEGIS would feasibly have jurisdiction over violations of more than 200 categories of crime, and operate at least sixty Legal Attaché offices and fifteen sub-offices around Heropa.

AEGIS's main goal, according to the pitch, would be to protect and defend the City of Heropa, to uphold and enforce the criminal laws of said metropolis, and to provide leadership and criminal justice services to mayoral and municipal agencies and partners.

It would take the lead in combating criminal organizations and enterprises, along with violent crime, the paranormal, and superhuman threats.

A carefully squirreled away clause that mentioned the right to preemptively strike against possible future threats made the man's stomach lurch.

The ramifications of such an organization were enormous, not least likely infringement on human rights and due process.

In the paperwork, Kahn also discovered who had been offered the role of executive director: his superintendent Rick Stoner – little more than a bullying would-be fascist, rumoured to have ties with the underworld fraternity.

Said executive director's principle role would be as subordinate to a twelve-member council (the membership of which would remain anonymous, empowered above and beyond City Council), and the fact that this AEGIS organization might operate as much as a covert agency as a quasi-military one, worried the police officer further still.

The whole damned thing made him rinse his cup, and turn to whiskey.

brigit

31

While she whistles Cole Porter's *Who Wants to be a Millionaire*, Brigit cleans her *bébé* like there's neither tomorrow *ou la journée d'après* – doing a spit and polish minus the saliva.

She'd started out with a cloth soaked in sewing-machine oil that was lobbed over her shoulder once it took on a slight colour of *poivre rose*, bearing a grittier feeling to the touch.

Some ignorant people, mostly men, called the Beretta a woman's gun.

Which is precisely what this was (hers), and yet these *hommes* carried on as if the weapon might be inferior, perhaps a toy. Or, worse, possess some kind of *infection sexuellement transmissible*, a venereal disease.

The bigger the shooter, these stupid men believed, the more respect and perhaps safety from *risque de contamination*.

Next up, Brigit had employed a fat, twelve-inch pipe-cleaner, pimping this in and out and then a wee bit more for good measure, twisting *et tournant*, doing ninety-degree rotations with what began as deft flicks of the wrist but degenerated into something akin to *un* swirl *désinvolte*.

Wasn't sure *un cure-pipe* was the best tool – surely there existed more professional ones – but it served its nefarious purpose and her old boy was looking dolled-up and sprite by the moment.

Since it had relatively minor recoil and a low level of noise, the Beretta 950 Jetfire must surely, therefore, be *inférieur*.

She still recalls a comment made by Goose Howard when he first appraised the pistol in his boss's new girlfriend's hand – *et passait pour un crétin.*

"A great little gun for senior citizens, especially elderly women who would have a difficult time pulling back the slide of an automatic pistol."

Pah. *Un raté total.*

Then Brigit swabbed a fresh rag with more of that machine oil and wiped down the exterior surfaces, giving them the kind of love and attention she'd wasted on few flesh-and-blood males, Sol being *l'exception.*

There had been better, more functional *revolver et pistolet* churned out on rotating industrial belts since this one first reflected *lumière du jour,* or nighttime luminous-tube signage, on the metallic surface of his skin.

But a weapon like the Beretta proved the skill of its owner.

With the sights on the Jetfire not being persuasively good, one had to rely more upon eye, balance and intuitive *jugement.*

The 950 was also hardly as easy to shoot as it looked to be. Its unconventional design took a bit of finessing before it became *un ami* to the handler.

And it could be mischievous; *c'est un vilain garçon... mais je l'aime bien!*

If a round in the chamber misfired, a tap-rack-bang manoeuvre only resulted in a double-feed jam, because there was no claw extractor to yank an unfired case from the chamber when racking *le coulisseau,* the slide.

Still – it might not be a Magnum powerhouse, but this *pistolet de petit calibre* could kill. The ability to fire nine rounds in a couple of seconds, with a short trigger pull, made the little gun far more reliable than many of its *gros calibre* brothers.

For face-shots, there was nothing better.

It was amazing, the damage made by a .25, upon penetrating a person's *crâne humain,* the skull – so long as the bullets used were hollow-point Fiocchi 50 gr FMJ.

The barrel is something *élégant.* Brigit uses a silicone cloth to wipe off fingerprints after all the manhandling.

She then examines this cheeky boy in the light from an overhead fluorescent. She might have ceased whistling M'sieur Porter, but says a few words aloud from his song, "'Cos all I want is you," and pats the gun.

And then she considers *la damselle*.

This girl was still in hospital, it had been a month, and according to reports she had not regained consciousness. *Se rétablir?* Perhaps.

When Bob Dukes suggested to Sol sending someone into the ward to smother her while she lay thus incapacitated, Brigit had slapped him three times across the face. *Il était au bord des larmes,* blubbering and sooking. Weep all he wanted to, her mind had been set.

For here rested a woman *croiser le fer avec*, to cross swords with, at the right time – when she was capable.

Non, Brigit would wait, and prayed nightly, clutching rosaries, for the *chienne* to recover.

Around her now, in the faux storage space that Sol used for meetings of *le gang*, its members shuffled and whispered, more restless than ever. Goose Howard was scowling while he played the *Anglais* version of *vingt-et-un*, blackjack, with three partners.

Everyone on edge since five of their number had been slain in a police raid. All of them self-important boys with big guns and small... well.

Brigit glances over from the chaise longue to her lover, who is sitting patiently in a corner, legs crossed, with a cheroot in his fingers and a copy of the day's paper before him.

"Sol, in English, when we talk about the penis, but more than one, *pluriel* – you know?"

"I know."

"*Bon.* So I have the question – do we say 'penises' or 'penii' – or 'pene'?"

"It ain't Latin, darling." He smiled indulgently. "Penises will do nicely, thank you very much."

little nobody

32

Don't let the pitter-patter of tiny footsteps deceive you – to me, they come across like the stomping of King Kong.

The Big O'd given me a mission, flying solo, 'cept I didn't have wings. Now here I stood cringing in the huge shadow of a terror that made *clickety-clack* noises as it waved antennal clubs about.

For real?

This is how you get your arse kicked. And maybe things were looking a little shady. Tell the truth, I wasn't enjoying it much either – this guy'd clearly decided I'm today's short crust pastry.

I manage to get a hand on one mandible apiece, trying to keep them from tearing me apart.

And all I can think is that I was a bonehead – I'd exhausted my one power restriction (Heropa's rules) on the ability to shrink down to a size one-third of a pea. I therefore wasn't able to pull a Hank Pym and control insects.

So what would you do? Me, I got down and dirty to use my fists, which would probably have as much effect as a pea-shooter taking on a Panzer tank at the Battle of the Bulge. Put all my weight – about 0.06 grams at this size – into a goddamned hopefully pile driver punch, which I swung at the enormous left eye after shouting a superhero-required, "Say cheese!".

Flashback: yesterday.

Teen Crusaders HQ.

Me hanging out with a couple'a buddies, Funk Gadget and Slam-Dunk Ninja – trying (and failing) to impress new girl Prima Ballerina. I swear I saw her roll eyes behind the domino mask while we blustered and hen-pecked one another. Hell, we were bored and restless, and girls are a mystery to me.

Precisely when we got a call from the bona fide boys at the CCC. On our monitor screen appeared head and shoulders of Sir Omphalos, making us cease carousing and stand in awe. Funk Gadget actually saluted, the idiot.

"Kids," the Big O said, "I need a favour."

This caused Gadget to whisper an expletive in my ear. "Shush," I responded.

See, the thing was, we were newbies.

Freshly arrived in Heropa, baffled and lost. We three boys'd banded together as would-be-heroes, doing mostly Capes-for-contract work, all lads as I say, so no Wasp to muck about with or win over – not until Prima arrived on our doormat, one on which Slam-Dunk had tactlessly inscribed the words *Beat it, Hippie*.

Started our own amateur Cape posse even though all four of us aspired to join the Crime Crusaders Crew, or their arch rivals Capitol Hill's mob. The CCC had local kudos, major players in a large urban sand pit we too were hell-bent on trawling.

Basically, however, our Teen Crusaders remained on par with the Teen Titans, way beneath everybody's radar – which made Sir Omphalos granting us a personal call something bloody extraordinary. I swear Funk Gadget wet his pants. Slam-Dunk feigned indifference, Prima acted like she didn't know what the fuss was about, and me? My dream was about to be realized.

When the big man begged us for that favour, and then signed off, we briefly broke out party blowers – later sitting down to nut out who'd be the lucky bugger to rep for our team. The only way we could decide who'd get said glory was by drawing Slam-Dunk's chopsticks, since we didn't own any straws.

I got the short one. While I whooped it up at the time, I now wondered how soon it would be before I said my prayers.

My singular knack? An ability to shrink to tiny size.

I'd grown up with vintage issues of Stan Lee and Jack Kirby's

Tales to Astonish featuring Ant-Man – they belonged to my granddad – and reruns of an old TV show called *Land of the Giants*. So I designed myself a red bodysuit based on Kirby's initial Ant-Man from 1962, with blue gloves, boots, and trunks. Had it made with fabric composed from that comic book reliable, unstable molecules. I even built an Ant-Man helmet out of papier-mâché, complete with antennae. These antennae, however, were sadly not functional. They were decorations that held no sway over bugs, meaning the first occasion I actually did reduce myself – today – I got into a diabolical fix.

The hero's moniker I chose was Little Nobody.

Don't worry, I've already decided it's goofy too. Reason for the decision came down to being rushed – I was kind of at a loss prior to downloading into Heropa. I mean, I had my repro Ant-Man costume idea, but a name? Nope.

Incidentally, the day before, I stumbled across a suitcase full of ancient twelve-inches that'd also been the property of my gran. We were cleaning up his stuff after he got Relocated to a Hospital. Anyway, seems he used to moonlight as a techno deejay/producer under the handle of Little Nobody. Sure, you can't play vinyl these days, so I dunno if they're good or shite – but the sobriquet stuck.

A neat word, sobriquet. It was the name of one of those LPs, so I looked it up.

Yeah, anyway.

An hour before I shrank down to encounter mayhem, Sir Omphalos had couriered over his only clue: a profile picture of a drop-dead lush blonde. While we three lads crowded round to ogle, Prima Ballerina huffed and practiced pirouettes.

On the back of the photo was scribbled the name 'Jean Dupont' – a pseudonym, or I'm a monkey's uncle – and a stamped company name and address for 'Ray-Man Studios'.

Not much to run with and I was hardly a detective, but I had my lead – and who'd skip out on their big break?

The studio address would do for now.

So I went outside, smiled to myself, and effected the chronic weight-reduction biz for the first time.

Bloody programmers back in Melbourne could've warned me.

Surrounding city buildings loomed tall as Mount Everest, blotting out the sky. I suddenly felt very small, while everything else was insanely big.

Jump-cut to Bizarro World – some things strange (dandelions being tall as trees? Oh, come on), a few horrible (like bees the size of double-decker buses), and others... not (well, peering up women's skirts, for prime example).

I had to leap about avoiding the footfall of complete strangers. Their steps, with shoes big as battleships, shook the ground and would spell instant pancaking if I didn't pay attention.

I also never realized before how dirty people were. Being forced to weave through cigarette butts the size of boulders and big lumps of discarded gum became a pain in the neck, when you're already craning to ensure no one steps on you.

And then, after an hour of this, on the edge of a city park that'd give the continent of North America a run for its money, I ran slap-bang into my guy: a garden variety ant, out for his constitutional.

Anyway, to bring you up to speed, slugging it out with my newfound six-legged friend was never going to amount to much.

Lucky, then, that I remembered I had a utility belt. Since I was no scientist, it had zero fancy gadgets, but housed snacks that shrank with me. Figuring the ant preferred processed sugar to unrefined Cape, I lobbed a bite-size Cherry Ripe in the opposite direction. While he scurried off to tea, I fled.

One problem down. A million others to go.

Like being stomped on by those hundreds of oblivious pedestrians, dodging lit cigarettes like Roman candles, and the act of actually traveling. With my tiny legs, it took another hour to cover just fifty metres. This shaped up as one very, very long day.

Most humiliating was getting caught in that park I mentioned by this kid with a net, and then imprisoned in her bug-catcher. The girl wandered off to leave me banging away, sandwiched on a picnic table between Birthday Barbie, who was a hundred times my height, and a surprisingly svelte Miss Piggy doll.

Took me a third hour to kick and punch and scratch my way to freedom. Jesus Christ, I decided as I climbed down, heights not being my forte. I needed another life.

And so we come to ten hours after I set out.

I stand in supposed safety close by a wall, bent over and puffing. I'd give my eye-teeth for bed with breakfast somewhere less dangerous and exhausting. The sign is miles above me, reading 'Ray-Man Studios', but then I notice the added '2F'.

Crap. It's on the second floor.

Squeezing my eyes shut, I try a spot of prayer – for something, anything, to make this job easier. Upon reopening them, I'm blessed to find there's a patrolman leaning against the wall. It's a start, anyway. Time to climb the human ladder, and further pray I don't slip.

After reaching his cap, maybe the thin air makes me delirious, or at least reckless, since thereafter I indulge in chancy gymnastics, hopping from brick to pipe, and end up using a clothes line with assorted monstrous bras to propel myself (via somersault) through an open window.

Squatting to catch my breath, I've decided I'm not half bad.

The corridor around me looked like the Grand Canyon, and possessed the same population: none. And at least the floor was clean. So I sprint across spotless parquet in the direction of a partially closed door – since it sported the company name I was after – and slip through the gap.

Two giants occupy this vast interior office space.

One of them, a man in a sporty hat and tweed suit who smoked like a chimney, stood by the single window. Another guy, seated in a chair behind the desk, looked like a younger version of the priest from that geriatric horror film *The Exorcist*. What? My dad loved the movie – I'd been forced to watch it a dozen times.

It's the priest lookalike who speaks first after my unnoticed, unforced entry.

"You've done well, Brodsky," his voice booms. Talk about Word of God stuff.

"Nah," bellows the standing man, in a slightly softer manner, as he taps the brim of his hat. "Thank my doll Brigit and her boys."

In response, seated guy exhales like a wind-machine, says, "Don't go boring me with the details," and then clicks his tongue. It's downright deafening. "The payment has been transferred to your account, as arranged."

Our other man pounds out his giant cigar in an ashtray in which I could swim. "Pleasure doing business, chum."

"Don't make it a habit," the priest fellow warns. "And keep this entire matter under that hat of yours."

"Sure." Another cheroot burst into flame, smoke descending like fog. "Brigit says she'll take care of this Bullet Gal dame if she recovers, so don't you worry."

The man in his chair laughed, the volume making me duck for cover.

"I never worry, baby," he roars. "Now scram – you can show yourself out."

Okay, cryptic, I'll give you that. They were winding up, and obviously I'd missed the lead-in discussion – but I doubted my eardrums could have taken much more. Realized I'd better get out of that place before I coughed aloud or died from smoke inhalation.

Trouble was, the standing man had moved between me and the door, and the two engaged in small talk that hurt my skull.

Thankfully, I notice then the small air vent positioned at floor level nearby. When I say 'small', for me the aperture was this grand archway with a grille easy enough to slip through. Better to take the long, unexplored route. After diving in, I worked the pipes: filthy places covered in mold, grime, and awful balls of hair three times taller than me.

The final duct led, however, into open air in a back alley, with a drop just a few centimetres above terra firma. While that might sound easy, at my size I wavered before taking the plunge – onto an admittedly soft landing of dog do.

Stumbling out of the stuff, swearing and appalled, I wave a hand before my face to push away stench. Cue: a vehicle driving past the end of the alley, to toss up water from a puddle that took on tsunami proportions. Before I could take cover, I got swamped and washed several centimetres, screaming all the way.

All right, so I no longer smell quite so much like poo, but am drenched in every other street-level aroma. Enough of toiletries.

Dripping and miserable, I locate a telephone box round the corner.

It takes me thirty-five minutes to climb up.

If anyone ever tells you it's easy to hot-wire a phone when you're barely bigger than a flea, given them a swipe from me.

As for lifting the receiver and dialing?

Ye gods.

mitzi

33

In a mirror attached to the hospital room wall, I gazed at myself.

The face returning this look was awfully pale, but outside the powder-blue gown there existed no sign of any damage, aside from two Band-Aids crossed like a wannabe Jolly Roger on the left side of the forehead – meaning the right side in reality.

"Funny," I remarked. "I don't remember my head getting injured."

In the reflection, behind me, Lee switched from glowing to sheepish. "That was me."

"Say again?"

"Last week, one of the days I came to see you, I accidentally clocked you with a briefcase as I brushed past."

"Gee. Thanks."

"It was an accident."

"Mm-hm."

"And you were unconscious. I didn't think you'd mind."

"No? Huh."

Beneath the hospital frock was where harm lay. The muscles felt stiff, and pain remained in spite of morphine.

Vaguely curious, I asked, "How long was I out?"

The looking-glass Lee slouched as he spoke. "Just over four weeks."

"Am I supposed to be alive?"

"No one else expected it."

"But you did?"

His eyes caught mine in the mirror. "I hoped."

That made me smile, even if it was difficult to pull off. Not because of the aches or how close I'd come to assassination, but since my facial features had had nothing athletic to do for a month.

Returning to the reflection, I saw that my brunette bob had grown out a bit and hung twisted and lank. "Why do you bother with that?" I said.

"With what?"

"Hair-growth. If I'm not real, I mean."

I saw him blink quickly. "You remember."

"Uh-huh."

"All right. I honestly don't know. I thought you'd wonder more about the pain."

"I've had enough of that in my time. I stopped wondering."

Funny how things go.

I'd been awake two hours before this Lee arrived.

Came to with a cute nurse poking a flashlight up close, and I almost decked the woman. Lucky for her, I couldn't even move for a quarter hour.

Making me captive audience when a middle-aged doctor entered. He was wearing a white coat and Groucho Marx moustache, with a more laughable head mirror above that. The man's name was Hackenbush.

This doctor sat on the edge of the bed to begin posing vacuous questions; mostly I think to make sure I might still be sane. He and a different nurse, a frumpy old woman referred to only as 'Matron', eventually raised me to a sitting position. The two of them continued fussing and chatting, and graciously shot me up when I complained of soreness.

Made me thrilled when they finally left.

This gave me time to mull over everything as it came filtering back.

And then?

I cherished the fact I could still breathe.

Looked around, appreciating the moment. There was a vase with fresh red roses on the bedside table, next to various jars of pills. On the wall above the cot someone had taped a vibrant print of a surrealist painting, the text beneath which said *Woman with a Flower, 1932 by Pablo Picasso.*

When Lee arrived he virtually ran in, behaving agitated – though in a happy way. Sharply dressed in a suit and neckerchief paired with a pocket square, he had a silly grin and clapped hands.

Helped the girl to her feet, steadied balance, and then placed me before the mirror so I could get narcissistic.

"By the way," Lee said from behind, "you're dead."

I glanced his way, narrowing eyes. "Well – that's put a dampener on things. Ouch."

"I mean dead in a good way," he hedged.

"There's a positive spin on the thing?"

The man rubbed his chin, putting on airs. "To my mind, yes."

That made me pull up my gown, showcasing jagged lines of stitching around my midriff, still on the mend. "And the pretty scars are bonus extras?"

Surprisingly, Lee didn't recoil. "Mitzi, you're lucky to be alive," he said. "At all. Besides, everything going smoothly, those scars will be a thing of the distant past."

I'd had enough navel-gazing in the looking glass. I turned slowly, cautiously (things still hurt), and examined my visitor more closely, murmuring; "Now you're losing me."

His response?

The arsehole beamed, his face lit up. "That, Mitzi, is the funny part."

lee #3

34

He said, "That, Mitzi, is the funny part." In an ironic way, he intended.

Unable to fathom how joyful he was to see her up and about, alive, thinking, throwing sly quips back his way. Worse for wear she might've looked, drained, ridiculously pale, but the girl didn't act like any of these things. Her emerald green eyes had a sparkle he could not begin to comprehend.

"Well, Jeez, Lee, don't keep me in suspense," she mutters, touching the somehow charming crossed adhesive strips on her forehead.

"Never the intention."

She now pushes annoyed. "Not saying it was, but I seem to've woken up grouchy."

"Mitzi," he assures, "given that you were recently riddled with bullets, this is hardly surprising."

"I'm not fishing for sympathy."

"And I'm not giving it."

"Swell."

"Welcome back."

"Ta." The girl leans back against the wall with crossed arms. Obviously exhausted, but covered well. "So what happened to this 'funny' business you made a song and dance about a moment ago?"

"What, am I now allowed to speak?"

"Always, m'dear."

"I think I preferred you unconscious."

"Easier to whack me about?"

"That was an accident. I said—"

"*Blah, blah.* I could do this all day."

"I know you could."

She smiles. "But I don't think you have the stamina."

"Listen, you're the one held together by pain-killers."

"Guess."

That's her cue to head over the bed and sit down, drawing legs up beside.

"Are we done with the post-op histrionics?" he inquires.

"Maybe."

"How do you feel?"

"Like death warmed up." She shoots him a warning look. "No quips, okay?"

"Never my intention."

"What is that – your stock phrase?"

"Not that I know of. I could be wrong."

"Yeah, right." Wriggling the fingers of her left hand, staring at them like they're someone else's, Mitzi sighs. "Can I ask a question?"

"Certainly."

"Who tried to kill me?"

Ah.

Lee thinks a moment, before reaching into a pocket and handing over a photograph, a copy of the one he gave to the Teen Crusaders. "This is her."

The girl receives the gift, stares it and again exhales, in a sad way. "She's beautiful." With one finger, Mitzi touches the profile in the photo. "What's going to happen to her?"

He doesn't need time to consider. "Nothing." Decides to tag it with, "At all."

Head bowed, hair tumbling over her eyes, the girl takes this well. "Oh."

"But," Lee adds straight after, "she will be punished." Walks over to the cot to place a hand upon her shoulder. "I swear."

Mitzi's response comes across anaemic. "How?"

meeting of the lees

35

The meeting happened one week before – secretively again, this time in the formal setting of a board room. The place had a lofty ceiling, marble floor, and a window that filled in for an entire wall. Dominating the one opposite hung a full-scale replica of da Vinci's *The Last Supper* in a gilt frame.

A white baby grand piano stood to one side beneath the painting.

In the apex of this space, rotating above a large circular table, were four copper ceiling fans. Lengthy strips of pale crinkled muslin gauze, draped either side of the window from roof to marble, flapped occasionally in the artificial breeze.

Around the oak table had been placed half a dozen swivel chairs on castors, and slapped in this seating were six identical blond men in navy suits. They shared exactly the same size brown patent leather shoes, broad silk ties (a leafy jacquard design bearing little swirly branches), and silver cufflinks engraved with a Hydra of Lerna emblem – their illicit club code.

One of the club members had, however, removed his jacket and flung it carelessly over the back of the chair. The top button on his shirt was unfastened, tie loosened. He was quaffing beer, whereas his peers stuck with vanilla tea from a matching set of Imperial Dalton porcelain.

"Must you drink at this hour?" asked a man across from our beer souse.

He saluted. "Fucking A."

"But it's eleven in the morning."

"So?"

A third member, sitting slightly apart from the others, rapped the table with knuckles. "Order," he announced. "Are we ready to continue?"

Another of the Lees stifled a yawn to his left. After a brief glare, the speaker resumed.

"Next on the agenda: What *are* we going to do about that phony – Mitzi?"

Which was when a fourth Lee leaned hesitantly forward, saying, "Excuse me, sorry, but can I say something?"

"You, Number Two?"

"...Yes? Is that a problem...? I can shut up, if you'd prefer."

"No, but I do wonder if surprises might never cease. Go on, then."

"Thank you."

The third Lee to have spoken, the one slightly apart, attempted an encouraging smile via a narrow slit of the mouth. "Let's hear it, Two." He then tapped his watch.

"Yes. Gentlemen, okay, we – I think we won't have to do anything."

The other Lee drew back a fraction. "How do you mean?"

Lee Number Four swore, finished his beer, and then huffed. "Pretty obvious, isn't it? I thought we had Brodsky's people handling the matter."

Our hesitant speaker moved his head from side to side. "No, no, I just mean – she's dead."

Everyone looked his way now, a couple surprised, the remainder upbeat. He feigned shyness under collective scrutiny.

"The devil she is," murmured the table rapper.

Number Four, clutching an empty bottle in both hands, had taken to chuckling. "Oh, what a fucking tragedy," he squeezed between peals.

"A genuine shame," said another of their number.

Four parked his mirth. "Don't give me that hypocrisy, Six. You couldn't possibly give a shit."

"Hah!" inserted Lee Number Five, all smiles. "Agreed. It's a blessing. Good riddance to bad rubbish."

"Still," said Number Six, "nothing to laugh about."

The worrisome member, the one who'd made the announcement, having straightened his lapel, began to unnecessarily fix his tie, face touching upon pink. "Please – don't argue."

Lee Number One knocked at the table again, sharply this time, still staring at him. "How did you come by this information, Two?"

The man jumped. "Which information?"

"Ding-dong. That the bitch is dead."

"*Um* – You know…"

"Pretend I don't."

"Well, whatever our feelings – it is official. I – Well, I read it in the *Port Phillip Patriot* this morning." Number Two shrank back. "Yes, yes, I know that's not enough, so I, *er*, called the hospital, and they confirmed it."

Nodding, Lee Number One also had a faint leer. "I see. Good work, Two. This saves us a spot of bother."

mitzi

36

Really can't be blamed that I gawked at Lee. "You did what?"

"I told them Mitzi was dead."

"Yeah, I heard that bit. Me, I don't understand how you scored yourself an invite."

"Incredibly? Sitting in on one of their clandestine meetings turned out to be a cinch."

"Because you're dead-ringers for one another?"

"Don't fool yourself. We can pick the difference."

I climbed to the edge of the cot, very carefully. Had pins and needles in my leg, the one that'd been shot.

This man, meanwhile, paced the room.

"No," he said. Having taken off his jacket, he held up a single silver cufflink. Engraved on it was something like a menacing octopus, judging from distance. "I printed my own invite. Are you thirsty?"

I nodded, watching as he went to a portable cabinet, picked up a carafe, and filled two tumblers with water.

"I went into the meeting," he said, as he passed over one glass, "pretending to be Lee Number Two – one of the 'inconsequential' Lees you talked up a while back."

Me? I sipped at my drink.

He threw his down like it was a shot of something.

Licked lips, and frowned, mumbling, "I lied to you."

That got my attention. "Sorry?"

"You asked me once if we had numbers, and I said we didn't. We do. I'm Number Three."

I hopped down to cold lino, wondering if I could steal a pair of slippers. "Three's not so bad," I said, while looking about. "How did you decide who got which number?"

"We drew lots."

Glancing up at his face, I saw he wasn't joking. "Well. That's awfully democratic of you."

The man hung onto my gaze. "Your Lee was Number Eight."

"And you filled in at this meeting as Lee Number Two – right?"

"Yes."

"All these numbers could get confusing." Having poured a refill with a surprisingly steady hand, I drank half the glass, placed it down, walked over to my visitor, and undid his neckerchief. "Where was the real Lee Number Two during this time?"

"Two's a very trusting man. I felt terrible tricking him, after he agreed to see me. We went for drinks. During this meeting the following morning, Two was sleeping off a mickey I slipped him."

I threw Lee's neckwear onto the bed. Placed my hands back on his chest.

He peered down at them with a mix of apprehension and distrust, said, "What are you doing?"

"Oh, I think I'm beginning to like this recent off-colour nature of yours."

"I noticed you stopped calling me Jeeves," he mumbled uncertainly.

"That riff? It got tired."

My fingers slid to his shoulders, where unexpectedly he winced. That seemed to make up the man's mind. He grasped both my wrists, shook his head, and then lifted and carried me back to the bed.

"Better not over-exert yourself, Mitzi."

Perhaps I would've pouted if there were any chance he'd believe the gesture, but I doubted it. So, instead, I oh-so-casually pulled up my gown to just below the bust, in order for him to glimpse again scars above my undies. Pretended the skin around was itchy. Pitching for the sympathy card, you see.

Don't know why I bothered. Blame the morphine, or the cheap thrill of finding yourself alive when you ought to be dead.

Lee's response was to lean over, gently pull down the material, and say, "Stop scratching."

Party-pooper. But that was okay, since I was suddenly feeling zonked-out and lay on my back. The man placed a cotton sheet over me, sat down in a chair close to the right, and squeezed my fingers.

"I'm so glad to have you back," said he.

My eyelids felt like dead weights. "That's what I don't get," I responded, staring up at the white ceiling with its tubes and wires, yet not seeing much at all. Realized I was completely vaguing.

"Mitzi," I heard Lee say, leaning closer, "there are two more things I need to tell you – things I learned at the meeting and from a friend."

That made me blow out hard, pushing away sleep, and I sat up too fast – causing a stabbing pain in my gut. "*Ouch!*"

"Are you all ri—"

I raised a hand in his face to shut the man up, warned him, "Uh-uh. Shush." Moved my torso very carefully, into a position where I didn't hurt quite so much. "Cigarettes," I demanded.

"Mitzi, we're in a hospital."

"So? In this day and age doctors smoked like chimneys." I frowned up at him, and since he was hovering again I squeezed his cheek. "Please? I need a ciggie – I mean, before you break me any more doozies."

"I don't smoke."

"Then find someone who does."

That settled it. Lee growled a bit, pulling his jacket back on, and sauntered out into the hospital proper. Had no idea how long he'd been gone, but he seemed to reappear five seconds later. I presumed I'd passed out sitting up.

"Here," he muttered, tossing a packet onto my lap.

I'd never seen the brand before. There was a man's head in a sea captain's hat, and the name Paul Jones. "These any good?"

"You tell me. I haven't the faintest idea."

"Fair enough." Unwrapping the pack, I then eased out one of their number. "Light?" A match flared before my face, almost singing my brows. "Careful, tiger." I dragged deep, and exhaled a cloud toward the roof. Not bad.

"Look," Lee interrupted, "should you be smoking at all?"

"Let me see," said I, tugging at my lower lip, feeling the beginnings of a nicotine rush in spite of all the other chemicals in my system. "I got shot five times *and* I'm a fictional character in a dumb video game. That makes me pretty much invulnerable."

I blew out again, glanced at Lee, and winked.

It was Lee's turn to sit down. He crossed legs and arms, body language all wrong, and stared my way with an expression I couldn't read, so I stopped trying. Leaned back instead to enjoy the fag.

After butting out the end of the cigarette in a stainless steel kidney dish, I began on another.

"You mentioned two things," I reminded my man.

"Yes. I did." Lee waved aside smoke. "I'll be brief. From what I understand, the other Lees were behind the attempted hit on yourself. And if you think that's bad, the next news is worse: they're going to hit Reset on Heropa."

In that moment I decided my nails needed a trim. "Ah. That old threat."

The man looked shocked. "You're aware of the Reset?"

"No, just me being facetious." The word hung there with fairly obvious ramifications. "Still – I'm presuming this Reset thingy may be my Kryptonite? Am I right?"

Lee rubbed a hand through his hair, looking fatigued.

"Honestly?" he said. "I don't know, since you're not a native."

"But you built this place," I pointed out, "well, you and your seven Photostats. Are you kidding me?" The cigarette dangled from my mouth as Lee peered at me slantindicular, yet said boo-hoo, and I took a long drag. "Wonderful."

lee #3

37

"To start with, I had a young associate do some checking – the job suited his particular superhero talent. Yes, a Bop, in common parlance.

"This fellow found out for me that Lee Number One is 'in cahoots', as they say, with the low-life that tried to murder you, or at least he is involved with her boss. A known felon named Solomon Brodsky. At this meeting last week, five of the other Lees confirmed knowledge and endorsement of the scheme. One or two sit on the fence, but they sanctioned it. *They sanctioned it.*

"The Lees' fingers are all over that particular pie, and I believe they in fact authorized and paid for same.

"Anyhow, they now think you're dead – which suits us. I convinced Gypsie-Ann Stellar, that reporter from the *Patriot* (remember her?) to run with a fake obituary.

"We have that different problem, however.

"Number One has convinced my brothers to hit Reset on Heropa, as I say, with the cycle then repeated every twenty-four hours. The thinking is that things here will be far more to their liking, more – manageable, I suppose. The population of Heropa, the 'phonies' as the Lees like to call them, start off from scratch nightly, the day's memories erased, without an ability to develop beyond initially-programmed personalities. Whatever personal evolution has been accomplished will be... negated.

"They're going to kill all chance of growth and individualism.

"And I can't stop them. They have the creation codes. I don't. Not yet.

"Yes, this might sound doom-and-gloomy, I agree, but I learned something else. The other Lees have a cheat-mode installed – a separate channel whereby people of their choosing are exempted. They don't have to suffer through the Reset."

mitzi

38

The speech floored me – yep, me who'd been shot five times. Lee's head had been downturned the whole time, eyes closed. It can't have been easy, I knew that.

"So you're saying a get-out-of-jail-free card," I suggested.

Still he shut me out.

"Go on." No answer, aside from muffled doctors' announcements outside the closed door. "Hey. You have a captive clientele here."

He looked up then, under his brow. "I know." Were his eyes moist? "Seems they also have their attention on a certain university professor. Reckon he might be useful to their cause. That's why they slipped in the escape clause."

"Is he?"

"Useful? I don't know." Lee lifted his chin and sighed. "It's a character roughly based on Abraham Erskine, the man responsible in *Captain America* comics for creating the Super Soldier Serum. Could be he's related in name only – one of the original Lee's passing fancies. But since they implemented the cheatmode, I piggybacked this process. Slipped in a few more 'phonies'."

Guess I hoped he'd say only one. I felt the need to be special, don't ask me why. I leaned over to sniff at the roses beside the bed.

"You know," I remarked, "that Matron woman said these flowers were exchanged for fresh ones every two to three days, the entire month I was off with the fairies. Who bothered doing that, d'you think?"

"I'm sure I wouldn't know," Lee Number Three lied.

He was terrible at it. His twins must've been ninnies to fall for the routine at that meeting of like-minds. Still, the thought he'd been so conscientious made me somewhat merry.

"Lee – Who did you add to the list?"

"You."

I laughed, keeping it short and sweet. "Of course. And?"

"A police detective I've liaised with. Some others that might prove a fly in their ointment."

"The reporter – Stellar?"

"No, not necessary there. She's actually a Bop. Like me."

This was news. "You've been busy, then. And here I've been giving you a hard time."

It was Lee's turn to chuckle. "One of your charms."

"Huh. I'm sure."

Walking to the window, the man slightly parted a curtain and surveyed a fake afternoon world beyond the glass. "There's one more thing I need to tell you," he said.

Think I groaned. If I did, it was timely. All these true confessions, straight after waking up from the sleep of the damned, were a bit much. I thought about complaining, but lit a fresh cigarette instead.

"Lee Denslow," my visitor began, still looking out the window, "is the name of my forebear in Melbourne. That's where we're from – the Lees, Gypsie-Ann, other Bops."

"Nice place?"

"A hell-hole. Nothing like this." He tapped glass. "One excuse for most Bops escaping to Heropa. Lee Denslow's reason was a tad different. You know he created Heropa?" Lee Number Three glanced over his shoulder, but thankfully there was no pride in his expression.

I responded that I didn't, and held off saying congratulations. The man returned to gazing outside. "As I say, this Lee

Denslow had his own agenda. He split into eight parts for good reason, looking for someone he'd lost, someone named Mina."

That comment kind of made me jump. Gained all my attention, at any rate. Found myself boring a hole into the back of Lee's skull. "Say again?"

"*Mina*. I'm not sure what she was to him. His wife? Former lover? Could've been a sister or daughter, or even a housekeeper. The details are murky. Anyhow, it seems the man deluded himself that he could resurrect her here." Lee closed the curtain. "But he lost track of the construct of his former paramour, or spouse, or friend. Hence us being created from the one, to make this search easier. And we lost our way. In many ways, Mitzi," here he turned to look at me, all serious, "I'm no more real than you."

I felt a chill, though the room wasn't cold. "So much for a brave new world. Huh."

lee #3

39

Silence prevails thereafter for at least three minutes, both parties fielding their own speculation. Lee parts curtains again to mark the beauty of a passing airship in the sky high above. He listens to Mitzi, behind, brushing out hair.

She needs rest, Lee understands that, but he would prefer not to end their conversation in such negative fashion.

"Listen," he finally says, "I have more."

Mitzi blows out cheeks, mutters, "You and your mores."

"Look, this isn't about breaking news. It's about what we – you and me, together – are going to do to fix things."

"Oh, very rousing. Am I supposed to give applause?"

"No, but a degree of patience would be appreciated."

Rounding on the girl, Lee tries his best to sound assured.

"So listen. In this world, I am a rich man. Perhaps only one-eighth of one – of a *man*, I mean – but I do understand right from wrong, plus I have the capital to fund anything we choose. I've decided, and hope you agree with me, to channel that money back into Heropa. A means of counteracting the damage being done here by my brothers."

Mitzi puts down her brush. "You make it sound so damned easy, Lee."

"Surprisingly? This might prove to be."

Moving quickly now, the man grabs a satchel he'd brought, swings a portable breakfast table over to the patient, and slaps documentation upon its surface.

"These are the technical drawings for a new building I've

designed – a beacon of hope and safety for the good people of this city."

Apparently nonplussed, Mitzi flicks through the material. "I thought you lot called us phonies."

"I'll never, ever use that word again." With a wave of his hand, he indicates a negative outline on blueprint paper. It looked from this angle like an elongated bullet. His nod to Timely Comics, the 1940s predecessor to Marvel. "This is it. Timely Tower."

"Nice name," the girl admits. "Marty Goodman'd be proud."

Lee shoots her a puzzled look. "You *get* the inference?"

"No biggie. Move on."

"Yes, well," he murmurs, still surprised, "I'm not certain Goodman is the type of tyrant I'd like to impress, but the homage to the publishing company and what they started is important." He rubs hands together, thinking it through. "Also, it's a poke in the eye for the other Lees who obsess more than myself over the golden age of American comics." Tapping a section of the building design, towards the top, Lee feels a sense of pride. "The Giant Map Room, here, is my wink to a better period – the silver age. Very F.F."

mitzi

40

The fact he was nerding-out came across kind of hysterical, but I preferred not to laugh – you know, in case I burst loose stitching holding me together.

"Okay," I said instead, "so you have a funky new building in the works. What's it for?"

"Our new headquarters."

That made me roll eyes, god help me. "The CCC rubbish again?"

"No."

Lee began to carefully place the papers back into his black bag – possibly the same one that'd crowned my forehead, leaving me wearing fashionable bandages.

"When the building is finished – which will be inside a week, before this Reset is timed to kick in – I'm going to call a press conference. I've had consultations with the other members of the Crime Crusaders Crew, except Major Patriot."

"So?"

He stopped packing, standing close to me as he was, and gazed down with an honesty that (almost) hurt more than five bullets.

"Trust me," was all he said.

That made me get up off that bed, unsteady as I might've been, throw arms about his shoulders, and tuck my face into the warm neck. "Okay."

I felt fingers strengthen cautiously around my waist, holding me secure, yet avoiding wounded areas.

"You're going to switch identities," he said softly into my hair. "The other Lees will continue to know who I am – of that I'm proud – but so far as Mitzi-slash-Bullet Gal? Well, she's checked out. We'll give you a change of hair-colour, a new alias, and no one here will be the wiser."

If it was possible, I snuggled closer. Eyes closed, breathing in light cologne and a tiny amount of sweat, I mumbled, "If I have to take on a new identity, can I fly?"

"No Cape can fly in Heropa, Mitzi. It's a cardinal rule."

"But you're one of the people making them, those rules," I insisted, holding him tighter. No escape, you see. "Go on – break this one for me. *Please?*"

"All right, all right. I'll see what can be done."

big game hunter

41

There's blood on my hands yet I'm well-nigh choking to death.

The weight behind me, somewhere I think near to my own, has that fishing line wrapped around my neck and is yanking hard. I've cut fingers up trying to stop the wire slicing further into my throat – I can see bone sticking out from the left thumb.

How long's it been since I gobbled down a last breath of oxygen?

Feels like hours, probably seconds. Passing out, I know – edges of everything blurring, head pounding, neck silently screaming on its sweet lonesome.

One thought fished in and out and around my head: someone knew the old secret identity and was trying to kill me in my own parlour.

Desperation dictates the next manoeuvre, a frantic shove back that sandwiches my attacker between me and a mantelpiece stuck over the fireplace. I hear the wind come out of him, the wire loosens the smallest fraction, and that's enough for me to stick my left hand through the garrotte and take pressure of the wire on my wrist – instead of further mutilating my fingers or my collar.

Gun. Where was the gun? Had no clue.

Still, the blurring folds in on itself and there's a moment of clarity. This is my time, I realize, one final lucky chance prior to giving up the ghost.

So I lift my right arm high and quickly hammer back with the elbow, praying to some empty mead hall of Norse gods that I get this right and nail the bastard holding me, rather than smashing up my funny bone on the concrete wall.

I'm lucky.

Hit something soft, and it's not a pillow.

The wire unravels from my neck, I swing round, and lob a haymaker right where the head should be. Only it isn't. This time I really do hammer the wall – feel a few knuckles crack.

"Goddammit!" I hiss a croak or croak a hiss, who cares which. Snap my left arm free of wire, and then cradle the busted-up mitt in fingers of the left hand while I hop up and down, trying not to bawl. Can still barely swallow and I gulp at air like a deranged guppy.

Funny. Can't quite recall when I remember about my assailant.

Once I do, I try to pull myself together and look to the floor.

There, spread-eagled by my shoes, is a small man probably fifty percent of my weight. I'd been amiss. Looked also half my height. From the state of his right eye, which had ruptured, I could accurately say my elbow had struck him there, instead of in the chest or stomach like I presumed. Messy. Currently out for the count, the bastard will need medical assistance and an eyepatch post haste.

Maybe I should stick him on a blind date with that cop Kahn?

Take my fine time as I try to clear my throat, making unpleasant sounds.

In addition, there's the fishing line at my feet to inspect. I hold the weapon aloft, looking past the bits of skin and droplets of blood. Superior piece of workmanship – a strong, braided monofilament core wrapped up in thick, waterproof PVC sheathing. The perfect weight and mass necessary to cast an artificial fly with a fly rod, and not a bad choice for doing a Gurkha on a Bop.

I measure the length and make some quick calculations. Wondering about strength versus weight contradictions, I flex the wire and pull hard. It cuts again into my fingers. Actually, there's blood everywhere, all over my safari suit and my boots. A lot of it mine, and I suppose I'll also need medicating soon enough.

I carefully roll up the line and stick it in my coat pocket, and then squat beside the dwarf. He's waking up. Hasn't yet realized he now has two-dimensional vision. There's one question to ask before I call in cops and rat out the silly prick.

I grab him by his shirt and yank him up into a sitting position. He swoons but anyway manages to focus the leftie my way.

"Any idea, sir," asks I, "what the bounty might be for my scalp?"

mitzi

42

At least they changed set location.

I was getting sick of exchanging dialogues in the same hospital room – it's not conducive to high drama.

Lee had me secreted to a private wing of the hospital, where the only medical staff allowed to see me were ones hand-picked by himself.

Thus I had to deal with Hackenbush and Matron, and these comedians insisted I be taken there in a wheelchair. Over the next three days they also ran about a million tests and started me on a crash-course of rehabilitation. I had the world's shortest hamstrings *before* I got shot, so didn't understand why they now coerced me to touch toes.

Was never going to happen.

Along the way over, I lost the Picasso picture, and gained an inane offering from Monet – some pond (again) with lilies on top. Joy.

Being busy with building blocks meant Lee popped in and out, and his remark about exactly how different hospitals in Heropa were from the Hospitals in his hometown (aside from the fact they capitalized the word there) didn't aid recovery either.

But I'd finally been granted some down-time from exercises, getting to sit alone in bed watching *The Honeymooners* on the box. Had asked Matron for pencils and paper that morning, and a few sketches were littered across the cot beside me.

When Lee strolled in, I immediately hid the hipflask of bourbon I'd pinched from Hackenbush's pocket – stuck it, appropriately, beside my left hip under the sheet.

"You're looking better," the man remarked, as he paced the small room, hands clasped behind his back. "More colour."

"Being slave-driven tends to have that result."

"Mmm."

Oh god, he wasn't listening. I resented when Lee did that. It meant my snappy dialogue went to waste.

Right now, he was sniffing the air. "Thought I smelled... alcohol," said he.

"You're in a hospital, Lee. Surprise."

"What? Yes – Yes, I suppose."

I decided to turn down the volume on the telly. "Are you all right?"

Since he didn't respond, I got out of bed (sneaking the flask under the pillow), put on a devastatingly gorgeous floral bathrobe, and intercepted the man. Made him cease the stomping by holding his arms.

When Lee ran eyes over me, he looked appalled. "What the devil are you wearing?"

"Standard-issue Matron."

"Jesus."

"Sit down," I said.

"Yes. Yes, you're right."

I pretty much shoved him then onto a vinyl armchair in the corner. While he sorted out whether to cross legs or pluck eyeballs, I poured us cups of black coffee thanks to an urn in the hallway. Sneakily added a shot of bourbon to both while Lee carefully folded his jacket and placed it beside him. His manners came in handy.

All that hard work also made me exhausted. I sat on the edge of the cot, watching him sip at the brew. Straight after, he decided, "Not bad."

"Thought you'd like it." I guzzled mine. "Now. Tell me this news."

"Yes, all right. Have I mentioned a press conference?" My nod confirmed this. "Ah. I did. Good. Well, I've been deliberating with the Great White Hope, Milkcrate Man and the Big Game Hunter. We've decided to shut down the Crime Crusaders Crew."

"About time," I said, right before drinking more.

"Perhaps. We have good reasons." Sadly, Lee placed aside his coffee unfinished. "By the way – if I need to get drunk, I'll do it myself."

I pursed my lips, mumbled, "*Oh.*"

"Now, back to the reasons. Number one, the Big Game Hunter has decided to call it a day here in Heropa. He's had enough. Probably the attempt on his life two nights ago made him reconsider."

Not sure how I reacted. I know I was surprised, and can't remember what I blurted out, but Lee simply held up a hand.

"He's fine. A few minor injuries, his ego more than anything. Anyway, this suits me – I have a job I'd like him to do for me back in Melbourne."

I wagged my head up and down, thinking this through. "Okay. That's it then. We're off the board. So what's the point of this Tinkertoy tower you're erecting?"

Rising to his feet, Lee walked closer. "The press conference is going ahead, Mitzi. But not to announce closure, no. To trumpet new beginnings."

Yeah, the man had a way about him in which he could pass off rousing clichés as, well, just plain rousing. I had to fight to repress a smile.

He then bent over, reached into his bag, and took out rolled paperwork. More plans, I guessed. Maybe he'd conjured up a Small Map Room to go with the big one.

Lee might not have debunked that notion with the disarming grin on his face, but did when he said, "This is for you."

Having removed a rubber band and carefully unravelled the three sheets there, he turned them over to show me by the light from the room's small Deco wall lamp. I'd say I lost my breath. God, I loved this man.

These weren't skyscraper blueprints – they were designs for a jetpack.

the great white hope

43

On the evening prior to the Reset, he sits alone in a darkened room, the only light source that of the city. Being alone? Nothing new.

Waiting for summons to the conference hall to play his part in a grand reveal.

Now, however, John watches the gridlock on the street several stories down – mostly reporters and photographers who scramble for parking – and wonders if this is such a good idea.

He hears Lee slip into the room behind before seeing him.

Doesn't actually need to look to claim confirmation – can tell by this particular brand of footfall that it's Lee Number Three.

So, still peering below at the traffic confusion, John says, "Are we doing the right thing?"

"Yes." Lee lets down a set of Venetian blinds to partially obscure that outside world.

"Easy for you to say," responds the Great White Hope, a little annoyed to lose light entertainment. "I can think of six reasons to reconsider."

Having claimed a stool by the window, Lee steeples fingers before his face – a thinking man's pose, but he made this decision long before. "Forget them," suggests he. "We've been over this already. Have no choice."

The other Cape leans against a wall, yet also doesn't. There's a one-inch gap between his pristine white cloak and the plaster. "You could leave," he says.

"No." Lee shrugs. "Not without the others."

"So you'll fight them instead."

"Someone has to. I mean, as of tomorrow they will have changed the bigger picture. Some things you and I don't care about – like swearing and drinking – will be abolished."

Chuckling, the Great White Hope stoops to pat his friend's shoulder, even if there's no actual contact. "Don't worry. The others will kick up an appropriate ruckus to make up for our indifference."

"And so they should."

Unexpectedly, Lee hops up and looks about the shadowy room, like he might find someone lurking there. When he spoke, he sounded calm, determined, if aggrieved.

"These are symptoms of a far greater crime: the Reset. Depriving Heropa's citizens of basic human rights, us deciding what's good for them – and what isn't. This makes the Prohibition feel like a tea party. A nanny-state with a hatchet."

"Lee," says his friend in a tone he attempts to make firm, "These are not real people. You do remember that?"

"No? Then what are they?"

The other man shakes his head, holds up hands, but finds nothing to add.

"Whatever they might be," continues Lee, "they live and breathe, feel and hope, love and hate. And they develop. We've seen that. You can't tell me you haven't. From midnight tonight, that's all going to change. Every twenty-four hours thereafter, memories get mined, experiences stripped – meaning they start over from scratch on a daily basis. We're stealing lives."

John might not have shared the man's passion for Heropa or its welfare, but he did admire it. That was why he stayed to help.

"I know." Begins again to plumb a grey area he's seen (of late) all too frequently, a fit of depression never far afield. "You *are* right. I get that."

In a light source blind-filtered through the window, Lee looks over and smiles. It's an honest expression he's good at – caring, concerned, yet trying to lift the mood. The perfect man to lead.

"Then what's the problem, John?"

"The problem?" The Great White Hope could list a baker's dozen: his fear, insecurity, the contempt and bitchiness of the rest of the team. Others he prefers not to go into. Sticks this evening to just the one. "I never asked to be second-in-command of anything."

"Well, now you are." Lee goes so far as to slap him on the back, though sadly flesh makes no contact with material. "I need you. I trust you."

"Why is that?"

"A better question is, why not?" Laughing, Lee moves toward the door. "Anyway, after tonight, the Crime Crusaders Crew won't exist in ongoing memory, fractional as it might be – but the Equalizers shall. Time to go, my friend. People to see, a public to appease and protect.

jimmy falk

44

The wood-paneled telephone booths in the lobby had each been seized. There was a queue snaking round the corner, made up of newshounds carousing, yelling, sniveling or sniping. Must've been over a hundred wild men here, and not a single girl.

The shouts were difficult to differentiate, but Jimmy gave it his best shot.

"Yeah, boss, I'm there now—"

"—don't care *what* other front page news you have lined up—?"

"But I lost my press pass, I swear!"

"—shitting me—"

"Bah... do you not *know* who I am—?"

"That's right!"

"—where?! *The press conference of the century!*"

"It's madness!"

"—you gotta lemme in—"

Jimmy tuned out further screams. Hands in pockets, he slouched about, hoping to find that Holy Grail: an unassailed phone.

Fat chance.

No, being a cub reporter meant he'd be shoved up the back of the line – pecking order, you know? – hence missing all the action in the grand ballroom next door.

This sixteen-year-old found an empty corner of the lobby, next to a maroon leather sofa. Sat on its edge, crossed legs, and tried enjoying the show. Journalists, he figured, would've done well in the Colosseum under Nero.

This was news, *the news*, in action. A moment of history, about to be grabbed, assessed, and disseminated by these men, these—

"Women."

The comment made Jimmy unbalance. He therefore slipped off the edge of the couch, and had to jump back in a hurry before a gaggle of correspondents stampeded.

Leaning against the nearby wall stood the person who'd startled him: Jimmy's boss Gypsie-Ann Stellar.

Thirtyish and deceptively small (5 feet 7 inches even in heels), Stellar wore a smart, box-cut tweed suit, with a little hat-and-veil number positioned (jauntily) on top of short hair. Hazel eyes watched her intern, and she had a wry expression.

Said, "Mustn't forget our girls now."

Staring back, the boy tried to pull himself together. "Sorry, Miss Stellar, but how—"

"Did I know what you were thinking?"

He hated when she did this, finishing his sentences, especially when those flourishes were incorrect. "Yes, ma'am. Are you – Are you some kind of mind-reader?"

"Nah." Gypsie-Ann removed gloves as she straightened-up on precarious pumps. "You're young, kid. You read like an open book."

Tossed one mitten his way, which he caught. Made her hurrah, at the same time that she pushed aside a reporter standing in her way, and then called, "To work!"

Bird-dogging star *Patriot* reporter Stellar was something Jimmy Falk had struggled with for the past three months, learning the trade as he went. During that time he'd been witness with her (from afar) of the rise and tragic fall of Bullet Gal – though Stellar had been following the Cape's upward trajectory for several months prior.

Now Bullet Gal was dead – and following on from the tragic loss, rumour-mill had it that the Crime Crusaders Crew was also history.

So why the flamboyance and secrecy surrounding tonight's press conference?

Jimmy shook his head – let Gypsie-Ann lose sleep over it.

The boy was merely a gopher, though a manservant likely got more respect.

No idea why, but Stellar had nicknamed him 'Olsen' and asked (repeatedly) if he wore a signal watch. She always laughed straight after, like it was some kind of obscure joke the woman refused to share. "Don't worry, kid," she'd sometimes add, wiping away tears. "It's the freckles, they make me nostalgic."

And the amount of times he'd been coerced into carrying shopping bags full of risqué women's undergarments?

Sometimes he believed he'd cry.

On other occasions, however, there was no possibly better teacher.

Stellar understood the paper trail better than any journalist he knew, wasn't always cryptic with her humour, she was generous, sharing, insightful, and damned smart.

So he put up with the nonsense.

Right now? He had something else on his mind, a legacy that belonged in a way to Bullet Gal.

Little Junie Mills might've been rescued from a human-trading racket, but the repercussions of that experience were clearly traumatic. At his slave driver's behest, Jimmy kept tabs on the Mills family, making regular visits.

Initially, he wondered why the boss cared.

Nothing further could be used in the *Patriot*, since Stellar quickly kyboshed the story – after it initially broke – to protect the victims involved.

So what was the point of weekly trips out to the folks' home?

That grudging appraisal had changed.

Thinks he now got what Stellar intended: for the boy to under-stand this six-year-old was a human being above and beyond the headline, and besides that a breath of fresh air. All in spite of the horrors she'd suffered. The kid deserved love, respect and privacy, not sympathy or hounding.

She also needed the steady hand of friendship.

During his stopovers, there arose moments when the child zoned out and saw beyond the present point. Likely remembering that kidnapping and the bloody way in which she was rescued. At these times Junie's parents dithered – at a loss – but Jimmy had a knack for dragging the child back by the bootstraps.

Tussled her hair, acted big brother, and turned this girl's mind to things a six-year-old ought to care about: toys, games, dress-ups, and comic books.

Eventually it transpired that when Jimmy and Junie and her parents sat in the living room for a round of Go Fish, or put on the radio to listen to Glenn Miller, he enjoyed this camaraderie of an accidental foster family.

Something that he, growing up in a state orphanage, had never met.

the aerialist

45

I scored my own dressing room.

Unreal.

The boys had to bunk together, so I guess being the single female had occasional advantages.

Once again, though, I was examining my face in a mirror – this one a long horizontal number surrounded by light globes.

Yeah, checking myself out'd become a disturbing habit, but show biz interfered and asserted its own hedonistic demands. Which explained why we were here, in a possible former strip show theatre, judging from furnishings.

Sir Omphalos had organized some big song-and-dance number to usher in the new blood – even if most of the stuff was old.

I told Lee karaoke was out. Yawn-inspiring speeches would have to do.

But this time, at least I was a redhead instead of a brunette, and Major Patriot didn't make the guest-list.

Marked the third occasion I'd 'majorly' changed hair colour (boom-boom). I barely recalled my native dirty blonde.

Or life in Nede, so long in the past.

I applied lippy in that looking-glass, using red liner and five coats of Guerlain Rouge Diabolique – an old Marilyn Monroe trick to emphasize the mouth.

Probably better now if I took lessons from Elizabeth I.

Then I peered over at the new costume, a kind of tight-fitting flight suit, hanging on the back of a door that was covered in cut-out silver stars. Turned to face a Rocketeer-style helmet, lonesome on the dressing table.

All right, at least this time they weren't (directly) plagiarizing from any single pre-existing costume. More a tribute.

Supposedly.

I returned focus to eyes in the reflection, doing liner, mascara and shadow to make me look less Mitzi. I also listened to the brouhaha of press-men outside, already crowding audience space before the stage. Wondered if Lee would allow me to unzip and accept cash in my bra.

Felt naked anyway without Dad's Star Model Bs, so I covered with a few sprays from a nice citrus no-name perfume I'd recently discovered.

Stay true, I told my hesitant doppelganger looking back. Always remember why you're here – to help decent people and stick dynamite up the others' arses.

Okay, Mina?

Okay.

the big o

46

Their press conference took twenty-two minutes and twelve seconds.

He timed it.

First up, former Cape institution the Crime Crusaders Crew was given the flick – without ado or shedding of tears – in less than one minute.

Introducing the concept of replacement group the Equalizers, along with the unveiling of their banner, took up a further five minutes and fifty-six seconds. Lee didn't let on that their logo was a monochrome mirror image of one belonging to the British Union of Fascists.

A three-minute slide-presentation showcased new headquarters Timely Tower, situated on an entire city block in Grand Midtown.

It took a further sixty seconds (or so) to introduce the Equalizers themselves: the Great White Hope, Milkcrate Man and the Aerialist, with he in the leadership role.

About ten minutes were lost to reporters and cameramen swamping the Aerialist, hundreds of flashbulbs popping and mics shoved in at every conceivable angle, seeking exclusive commentary from their single female member.

This made him laugh. He knew how much Mitzi would hate it – although when she toyed with the flight suit's zipper, an impish expression taking hold, he'd been forced to give her the eye.

Over the course of the twenty-two minutes and twelve

seconds, a single reporter thought to question what happened to Major Patriot.

More than two-dozen other members of the press expressed dismay over Big Game Hunter's departure and the tragic loss of Bullet Gal.

But every single one of them applauded when the replacement team departed the stage.

The Equalizers' debut, most people agreed, was a success – auguring well for an uncertain future.

Afterward, a private function took place in the lower penthouse suite of Timely Tower, amidst the smell of fresh paint and celebratory pennants and streamers.

To music provided by big band leader Cake Icer and his combo, a hundred-odd VIPs got themselves smashed on an open bar and whooped it up poorly.

While dancing might be allowed to continue, the flow of alcohol – for the Bops at least – would end tonight with the Reset.

Commiserating, and having guzzled far too many screwdrivers, Milkcrate Man threw up inside headwear and down his front.

Lee, with John, had helped the man to brand new quarters. Needed to strip soiled clothes – the Great White Hope pinching his nose while manhandling a coat he swore had never anyway seen a dry-cleaner's – and then they shoved this mostly-unconscious drunk beneath the shower. Toweled him down, switched to PJs, and finally tossed their luggage onto a bed with sheet atop.

In the gaps between songs, if you listened carefully, you could make out Milkcrate's snores.

It is now fourteen minutes before midnight and Lee – dressed in his Sir Omphalos rig – stands to one side of the reception area at Timely Tower.

He's observing a party (still) in full swing.

"I feel like Cinderella." Mitzi had made this comment as she slid up beside him. She'd needed to stand on toes and say it right in his ear, due to the nearby ruckus.

He glances at the redhead and smiles.

Surprisingly, she wasn't tight – even if she had not been forced to wear the new helmet as part of a costume she grudgingly wore. That was tucked, still, under the right arm. She'd cheated by applying a lot of make-up, in order that no one would recognize her anyway.

The woman has a glass of champagne in her left hand, but had been pacing herself.

"How do you mean?" says Lee.

"The midnight thing. The moment we lose all the magic."

In spite of the cosmetic façade, she looks blue.

"Mitzi, live a little. You can now fly, can't you?"

A passive nod isn't enough for the man.

Having checked the time, Lee places an arm around his partner's waist, whispering, "Don't be alarmed – I'm not getting frisky. But I do need to show you something."

Back to better form, Mitzi looks up at him, deadpanning, "Don't tell me you're abandoning such a wonderful soirée?"

Yet he marks that her arm has returned the friendly embrace.

"Come on, let's go," says he, navigating his charge through a mass of revelers in tuxedos, cocktail dresses, dominoes, and capes.

There's an entry marked *Private (Equalizers Only)*, which he unlocks, and they ascend a short flight of stairs. Lee removes his cowl and gloves, pushing them into his belt.

"You know your hair is flattened," Mitzi remarks.

"One of the hazards of wearing a mask."

Straight after, she slows a fraction, aware now where they were headed. "The rooftop? Seen it, and—"

Which is the moment he opens the outer door, and a soft, vibrant, gloriously artificial illumination floods everything.

"—*Oh*. Nighttime in the big city."

"Heropa at its best, no matter what is changed."

They step out onto the patio, surrounded by a forest of potted flora, making themselves at home on two comfy armchairs he'd previously arranged. Between them? A bottle of Bollinger on ice in a silver bucket, along with two flutes, a crystal ashtray, and one pack of Paul Jones.

Nearby, down several stories, skipped a gigantic pink girl (made from luminous gas-discharge tubes containing rarefied neon or another gas) dolled up with pigtails. Surrounding it were a horde of other animated neon signs, some with moving pictures and letters, like 'Grouchy Buddha's Cabaret', 'Bond's Two-Trouser Suits', 'IF?', 'Port Phillip Patriot', and 'Get Inked'.

Above a neighbouring Art Deco structure to the right was a neon marquee sign with large, illuminated red and orange letters in a timed sequence that repeated, 'H', 'HER', 'O', 'HEROPA', off. To the left, big spotlights with long beams swept the sky, occasionally uncovering passing airships.

Their soundtrack came courtesy of automobile traffic, the thump of distant propellers, and jazz filtering through from downstairs.

"We have ten minutes left in which to live it up," explains Lee, pouring drinks.

"Why, Jeeves, you shouldn't have."

Gazing straight ahead, he mutters, "Huh. *That* again," before sipping champagne. A hand then gently touches his shoulder, making him turn from the city spectacle.

Mitzi is watching the Big O, *sans* mask, rather than the lightshow. "You're not mad, are you?"

"Of course not." Lee breaks into another smile, noting the rainbow those nearby '40s commercial signs created as patterns across the girl's face. "It's a beautiful view," the man admits.

Finds he's unable, at that moment, to look away.

Yet upon hearing her return – "Not too shabby for a wire-and-mirrors job?" – Lee has to anyway roll eyes.

"Mitzi, just shut up and enjoy the performance."

FINIS.

SMOKING GUN GLOSSARY

Abraham Erskine: comic book biochemist & physicist; developed Super-Soldier Serum that created Captain America in 1941

Ace Rimmer: heroic & dashing Space Corps test pilot in *Red Dwarf*

Adams, Neal: American comic book artist famous for work at DC

AI: Artificial Intelligence

Akutagawa, Ryūnosuke: Japanese writer famous for *Rashōmon*

Alicia Masters: the Thing's long-time sculptor girlfriend in *Fantastic Four*

Allan Quatermain: hero of H. Rider Haggard's 1885 novel *King Solomon's Mines*

Animal Farm: George Orwell's 1945 novella

Ant-Man: Marvel hero created by Stan Lee, Larry Lieber & Jack Kirby in 1962

Arse: ass

Art Deco: influential visual arts design style popular in the 1920s & '30s

Arthur Conan Doyle: British writer who created Sherlock Holmes

Axis Powers: Germany, Italy, Japan & other allies in World War II

B&E: breaking and entering

Barre: handrail that provides support for people during exercise

Batman: character created in 1939 by Bob Kane & Bill Finger

Beretta: Italian firearms manufacturing company

Battle of the Bulge, the: major German offensive tank campaign 1944/45

Baxter Building, the: Fantastic Four's skyscraper HQ in Marvel Comics

Beano, The: long running British children's comic, first appeared 1938

Bialya: fictional country appearing in DC Comics

Big Sleep, The: 1939 hardboiled crime novel by Raymond Chandler

Biggles: James Bigglesworth, a fictional pilot and adventurer, written by W. E. Johns

Billie Holiday: American jazz musician and singer-songwriter

Binos: binoculars

Bizarro World: a fictional planet appearing in DC comics

Black Canary: DC hero created by Robert Kanigher & Carmine Infantino in 1947

Bogie/Bacall: Hollywood actors Humphrey Bogart & Lauren Bacall

Bollinger: French champagne house founded in 1829

Bop: Heropa slang for a Cape, or super-powered individual

Box, the: TV

Brave New World: sci-fi novel written by Aldous Huxley in 1931

Breakfast at Tiffany's: 1958 novella by Truman Capote; 1961 film adaptation

Brekky (slang): breakfast

Brolly (slang): umbrella

Bulletgirl: Fawcett Comics hero created by Bill Parker & Jon Smalle in 1941

Burke and Hare: 19th century British grave robbers

Bushidō: The Soul of Japan: 1900 book by Inazo Nitobe exploring the way of the samurai

Cape: super-powered individual, hero or villain

Captain America: Timely Comics hero created in 1941 by Jack Kirby & Joe Simon

Captain Freedom: comic book hero created by 'Franklin Flagg' in 1941

C. Auguste Dupin: character in Edgar Allan Poe's *The Murders in the Rue Morgue*

Charles Atlas: developer of a bodybuilding method famous in comic book ads

Chandler (see Raymond Chandler)

Cheroot: a cylindrical cigar with both ends clipped during manufacture

Cherry Ripe: a brand of chocolate bar manufactured in Australia since 1924

Christopher Nolan: English film director, screenwriter, and producer

Ciggie: cigarette

Clark Gable: Hollywood actor, famous for *Gone With the Wind* (1939)

Clod: idiot

Cold Comfort Farm: 1932 comic novel by English author Stella Gibbons

Cole Porter: American composer and songwriter

Colt (1911) .45: semi-automatic pistol produced by Colt from 1911

Corr!!: a British comic book launched in 1970

Cowl: hooded portion of a cloak or superhero costume

Daily Planet: fictional newspaper appearing in DC Comics; Clark Kent work there

Dark Knight: 2008 Batman film by Christopher Nolan

Dashiell Hammett: American author of hard-boiled detective novels and short stories, famous for Sam Spade & the Continental Op

Deco (see Art Deco)

Delahaye: French automotive company founded by Emile Delahaye in 1894

Ditko, Steve: comic book artist, creator of Doctor Strange and co-created Spider-Man

Doc Martens: Dr. Martens is a British footwear and clothing brand, est. 1947

Docs (see Doc Martens)

Dog do: dog poo

"Doing a Gurkha": strangling someone, typically with a garrotte

Domino mask: small, often rounded mask covering only eyes &

the space between

Don Wright: the alias of Captain Freedom

Duffer (slang): silly person

Dunny: toilet

Eisner, Will: American cartoonist, writer & creator of *The Spirit* in 1940

Elizabeth I: British Queen, 1559-1603

Erskine (see Abraham Erskine)

Escher, M.C.: Dutch graphic artist who made mathematically inspired woodcuts

Exorcist, The: 1973 horror film directed by William Friedkin, starring Max von Sydow

F.F.: Fantastic Four

Fag (slang): cigarette

Fantastic Four: fictional quartet created by Jack Kirby & Stan Lee at Marvel in 1961

Fiocchi 50 gr FMJ: Italian-made ammunition

Flash, the: recurrent DC comic hero with the power of super-speed

Flashman, Harry: 19th century antihero created by George MacDonald Fraser, based on character in *Tom Brown's School Days* (1857)

George MacDonald Fraser: Scottish author best known for his Flashman series

George Stevens: American film director, producer, screenwriter

Georges-Eugène Haussmann: renovated Parisian waterworks, commissioned by Emperor Napoléon III

Glenn Miller: American big band musician, composer & bandleader in the swing era

Golden age of comics: the late 1930s to the early 1950s

Gone With the Wind: 1939 Hollywood film starring Clark Gable & Vivien Leigh

Gotham City: fictional home to Batman in DC Comics

Graf (slang): graffiti

Gran (slang): grandmother or grandfather

Greatest Story Ever Told, The: 1965 Hollywood movie

Green Arrow: DC hero created by Morton Weisinger & George Papp in 1941

Greyhound: intercity bus service founded in 1914

Grimster: grim person

Groucho Marx: American comedian & film and TV star

Guerlain Rouge Diabolique: a lipstick Marilyn Monroe is rumoured to have used

Hall of Justice: home of TV's animated *Super Friends* (1973-86) & incorporated by the Justice League in DC Comics

Hammett (see Dashiell Hammett)

Handle (slang): name

Hank Pym: Marvel Comics character, the original Ant-Man

Have Gun – Will Travel: Western TV series that aired from 1957 to 1963

Hawkeye: Marvel character created by Stan Lee & Don Heck in 1964

Henri Gaston Giraud: French artist, cartoonist & writer better known as Mœbius

Hergé: Georges Prosper Remi, the Belgian cartoonist who created Tintin

Horse Feathers: 1932 Marx Brothers comedy

Hospital: spelled with an uppercase H, a form of prison in future Melbourne

Hydra of Lerna: a serpentine water monster in Greek and Roman mythology

Hylax: a huge future Melbourne corporation specializing in plastics

Ian Curtis: the late lead singer of British band Joy Division

Infantino, Carmine: American comic book artist & editor, a major force in the silver age of comic books

Ingmar Bergman: Swedish director & writer who worked in film, TV & theatre

Invalid Stout: beer brewed in Australia since 1909

Jack Kirby: American comic book artist & writer regarded as one of the medium's major innovators & one of its most prolific and influential creators

Jaguar D-Type: sports racing car produced by Jaguar between 1954 & 1957

Jeeves: Reginald Jeeves is a character in the humorous stories by P. G. Wodehouse, being the highly competent valet of wealthy & idle young Londoner Bertie Wooster

Jim Steranko: American artist, comic book writer/artist, historian & magician

Joe Simon: American comic book writer, artist, editor & publisher

Joy Division: English band formed in 1976, later known as New Order

Kawabata: Nobel Prize-winning Japanese author Yasunari Kawabata

Kipper: a whole herring gutted, salted or pickled & cold-smoked

Kirby, Jack (see Jack Kirby)

Knickers: underpants, briefs

Kon: Japanese film director, animator, screenwriter & manga artist Satoshi Kon

Kryptonite: alien mineral with the property of depriving Superman of his powers

Kubert, Joe: American comic book artist, teacher & founder of The Kubert School

Kurosawa: Japanese filmmaker Akira Kurosawa is regarded as one of the most important & influential filmmakers in the history of cinema

Land of the Giants: American sci-fi TV program from 1968-70

Lara Croft: fictional character & protagonist of video game franchise *Tomb Raider*

Latveria: fictional nation in Marvel Comics, ruled by Doctor Doom

Lauren Bacall: American actress famous for *The Big Sleep* (1946)

'Le Marseillaise': national anthem of France, written in 1792 by Claude Joseph Rouget de Lisle

Little Orphan Annie: daily American comic strip created by Harold Gray in 1924

Loo: toilet

LP: record

Louise Brooks: iconic American film actress & dancer

Madness and Civilization: 1961 book by French philosopher Michel Foucault

Magpie: character created in 2016 for Australian comic zine *Oi Oi Oi!* by Andrez Bergen with artist Frantz Kantor

Management Control Division: public organization responsible for the containment of Deviants in near-future Melbourne

Man of Steel, the (see Superman)

Man Ray: American visual artist who was a significant contributor to the Dada and Surrealist movements

Marilyn Monroe: American actress and model, star of *Gentlemen Prefer Blondes*

Martin Balsam: American actor best known for *Psycho* & *Catch-22*

Marty Goodman: American publisher of pulp & men's adventure magazines, and comic books—launching the company that would become Marvel Comics

Marvel: American comic book company founded in 1939 as Timely Comics

Mary Celeste: American ship found adrift and deserted in the Atlantic Ocean in 1872

Max von Sydow: Swedish actor, famous for a game of chess with Death in Ingmar Bergman's *The Seventh Seal* (1957)

Melbourne: Australia's second-biggest city, founded in 1835 by John Batman

Mickey: a drink spiked with drugs

Mishima: Japanese author, poet, playwright, actor & film director Yukio Mishima

Mizoguchi: Japanese film director & screenwriter Kenji Mizoguchi

Mo (slang): moustache

Mojo: magic power, superpower, or spell

Murakami: Japanese writer Haruki Murakami (*Wind-Up Bird Chronicle*)

Mysterion (slang): mysterious person

Mystery Men: 1999 American superhero comedy film directed by Kinka Usher

Nede: an offbeat doppelganger of the city of Melbourne in *Depth Charging Ice Planet Goth*

Nickel: five-cent coin

Nick Fury, Agent of S.H.I.E.L.D.: 1968-1971 Marvel comic book series

Noggin (slang): head

Olsen: James Bartholomew 'Jimmy' Olsen is a character who appears mainly in DC Comics' Superman stories

'Oo-oo, Mary Sue': song performed by Gene Clark, an American singer-songwriter & founding member of folk rock band the Byrds

Oshii: Japanese filmmaker, TV director & writer Mamoru Oshii (*Ghost in the Shell*)

Ozu: Japanese film director & screenwriter Yasujirō Ozu (*Tokyo Story*)

Panzer: a light army tank produced in Germany in the 1930s

Patriot (see *Port Phillip Patriot*)

P. G. Wodehouse: English author & one of the most widely read humourists of the 20th century

Phantom Corsair: prototype automobile built in 1938

Pitt, Stanley: Australian cartoonist & the first Australian comic book artist to have original work published by a major American comic book company

PJs: pyjamas

Port Phillip Patriot: mid-19th century newspaper published by

John Pascoe Fawkner

"Pull the other one": expresses a suspicion that one is being deceived or teased

Relocated: people sent to prison-style Hospitals in future Melbourne

Repro: reproduction

Raymond Chandler: American novelist & screenwriter most famous for hard-boiled detective character Philip Marlowe

Richard Boone: American actor who starred in over 50 films

Rosaries: string of prayer beads used in the Catholic Church

Salvador Dalí: Spanish artist and Surrealist icon

Samuel Butler: iconoclastic Victorian-era English author

Sazae-san: Japanese manga series first published in 1946

Scheffel: Mark Scheffel, a famous brand of binoculars

Seeker Branch: secretive organization in near-future Melbourne involved in the collaring and detention of Deviants

Seventh Seal, The: 1957 Swedish film written & directed by Ingmar Bergman

78s: flat disc records, made between 1898 & the 1950s, played at a speed of around 78 revolutions per minute

Sèvres porcelain: one of the principal European porcelain manufactures

'She's Lost Control': 1979 song by English post-punk band Joy Division

Silver age of comics: 1956 to circa 1970

Singin' in the Rain: 1952 American musical comedy directed by Gene Kelly & Stanley Donen

"Slagged off" (slang): insulted

Smallville: American TV series, 2001-2011, based on Superman's hometown

Soviet Formalism: a school of literary theory, art & analysis that emerged in Russia around 1915

Spider-Man: character created for Marvel by Stan Lee & Steve Ditko in 1962

Stalingrad: The Battle of Stalingrad, from August 1942 to February 1943

Star Model B: Spanish 9 mm pistol almost identical with the Colt 1911 .45, used by Samuel L. Jackson's character Jules in *Pulp Fiction*

Stan Lee: comic-book writer, editor, publisher, media producer, TV host, actor and former president and chairman of Marvel Comics

'Strange Fruit': 1939 song performed by Billie Holiday

Steranko (see Jim Steranko)

Steve McQueen: American actor, starred in *Bullitt* (1968)

Superman: character created by Jerry Siegel & Joe Shuster; first appeared in 1938

Ta (slang): thanks

Talbot-Lago: French automobile manufacturer

Tales to Astonish: comic book series published from 1959 to 1968

Tezuka, Osamu: Japanese manga artist & animator, created *Astro Boy*

The Exorcist: 1973 American horror film directed by William Friedkin

The Honeymooners: American TV sitcom, 1955-56

The Last Supper: late 15th-century mural painting by Leonardo da Vinci

The Running Man: 1987 American sci-fi film directed by Paul Michael Glaser

Thing, the: *Fantastic Four* character created by Jack Kirby & Stan Lee in 1961

Throbbing Gristle: English music and visual arts group formed in 1976

Timely Comics: earliest comic book arm of American publisher Martin Goodman, which would evolve by the 1960s to become Marvel Comics

Tinkertoy: toy construction set for children created in 1914

Toff: derogatory stereotype for someone with an aristocratic background

Tokarev SVT-40: Soviet semi-automatic battle rifle

Twelve-inch: vinyl record twelve inches in diametre

Undies: underwear

Vera Lynn: English singer enormously popular during the Second World War

Victorian: built or made during the era of Britain's Queen Victoria (1837-1901)

Victoria Police: law enforcement agency of Victoria, Australia, formed in 1853

War of the Worlds: sci-fi novel by English author H. G. Wells first serialised in 1897

Wasp: Marvel character created by Stan Lee & Jack Kirby in 1963

Who Wants to be a Millionaire: Cole Porter song

Willy: Penis

Wodehouse (see P. G. Wodehouse)

Wood, Wally: American comic book writer & artist best known for work on EC Comics' *Mad*

W6-class: electric trams built in Melbourne 1951-55

Andrez Bergen

FROM PISTOLERO TO POSEUR

Ever had a character that you can't seem to cold-shoulder – not that you have no idea how, but because you don't actually want to?

Deep down where it counts, I mean.

Mood-swings might shake the apple – we all know Conan Doyle chucked Sherlock Holmes off a waterfall, before reviving him eight years later – but the character weathers whims, and sticks his or her roots in to stay. Like all those different actors playing James Bond, I guess.

In my case, it's Bullet Gal.

She started out "life" simply enough – a member of the cast in my 2013 novel *Who is Killing the Great Capes of Heropa?* Bullet Gal, a.k.a. Mitzi (her last name remains a mystery), was basically a joint homage to Lara Croft, Buffy, Tank Girl and golden age comic characters Sand Saref, Miss Fury and Bulletgirl. She even snatched that

With these influences in mind, Spanish artist JGMiranda put together a pin-up that appears on page 181 of the novel.

Mitzi's pistols – polished-nickel 9 mm Star Model Bs, each with a mother-of-pearl handgrip (and in fact cheap Spanish rip-offs of the iconic Colt .45) – are the same one that Samuel L. Jackson flourished to ill-effect in the film *Pulp Fiction*.

Mitzi was everything right about a female character: strong, determined, street-wise, witty, and better than most of her male peers in spite of a horrific past. Anyway, all this guff aside, when I wrapped the *Heropa* novel, I thought I said farewell to Bullet Gal as well, and that made me sad.

Something of her must've stuck in my gullet.

I felt like there was more for Mitzi to say. This might explain away how, when I commenced my next novel (2014's *Depth Charging Ice Planet Goth*), which is a coming-of-age story in the 1980s, in a surreal, warped version of Melbourne – somehow

175

principle character Mina morphed into Mitzi.

I'm still not sure how she pulled that off. It ended up becoming a distant prequel to *Heropa*, set about five years before, and her offbeat origin tale.

Afterwards in 2014, I found myself in the unusual position of floundering without a book to occupy my brain.

The previous year I'd gotten stuck into writing comics and occasionally illustrating them.

Again, Mitzi clouded better judgement, demanding a twelve-issue solo comic book series that I made across 2014-15, doing words and Dadaist-style art on the fly, without any game plan, and published through IF? Commix in Australia.

This ended up being the filler story between *Planet Goth* and *Heropa*, a genre mash-up of noir, crime, pulp and sci-fi – and was a hugely successful, especially reviews-wise. Don't ask me how or why, but I ain't questioning.

The *Bullet Gal* comic book debuted in August 2014, and finished its twelve-issue monthly run in July 2015. We promptly bundled the lot together as a 345-page trade paperback published through Canada's Under Belly Comics the same year, re-released as a no-frills-version by Project-Nerd Publishing in the U.S. in May 2016.

Once I wrapped that series, I decided it was my Reichenbach Falls, Bullet Gal out of my hair. Believed I could safely move on.

Mitzi's story was told.

And yet.

Man, how many times have you heard that expression? 'And yet'. Anyway, *and yet* she lingered – meaning that this year Mitzi was fit to kick the bloody door down.

First up, I got the bug to revamp the twelve-issue series as a novel. Rewriting a comic as a book means a hell of a lot of extra effort utilizing narration, expanded detail, and verbal descriptors – since there aren't any pretty pictures. Whimsical goings-on like the ants (from #10) are a lot harder to shape in a seemingly more dramatic literary take, but I realized the nature of the comic, its dips from morose to comedic and on into surreal, all the while playing second fiddle to hardboiled noir, were possibly its strengths.

I also introduced new characters and settings, round out others, and completely revamped sections.

This novel, while intended as a standalone, precedes *Who is Killing the Great Capes of Heropa?* by about four years (Heropa time). It takes place a year after *Depth Charging Ice Planet Goth.* A reading of both books might add colour to the characters and world herein.

My first novel *Tobacco-Stained Mountain Goat* (2011) is set in the near-future, last-city-in-the-world dystopia that Melbourne has become, and will fill in the dots about Hospitals, Seeker Branch, Hylax, and Relocation.

Meanwhile, Mitzi'll be making a guest appearance in an Australian comic series I do with artist Frantz Kantor called *Magpie*, which is featured in national magazine *Oi Oi Oi!*

Fellow Aussie artist Graeme Jackson has also convinced me to revive her star as a guest in our upcoming comic *Crash Soirée.* In my initial script she was a maybe, possibly a cameo, but over the past few weeks Graeme and I put our heads together and conjured an heir-apparent.

It's been eye-opening legacy stuff, and makes me realize the Bullet Gal idea is something that's dangerously infectious, since Graeme shows all the same symptoms of infatuation. Together we also created Jimmy (James) Falk and refined Mitzi's costume.

Anyway, this Bullet Gal that he and I dreamed up isn't Mitzi at all. She's a bubblegum-masticating teenage "legacy" character named Junie Mills (her name's a doff of the hat to pioneering *Miss Fury* creator Tarpé Mills) that sent me scrambling back to the *Bullet Gal* novel manuscript to insert Junie's own origin – which involves Mitzi rescuing the six-year-old from a human trafficking ring.

Get it? Got it? Good. (That's a joint Basil Rathbone and Danny Kaye line I nicked from *The Court Jester*, 1955) Stay tuned for more guns, guts and (likely) mayhem.

Otherwise, I'd like to take a quick moment to thank people like Graeme (my first actual reader of the *Bullet Gal* novel manuscript), Brian (my best friend and himself the origin story behind Milkcrate Man), Giovanni, Merz Dada, Christopher TM, Lori, Ken, Galo, Iggy, Matt, Renee, Nat, Frantz, Olivier, Nath, Cristian, Steven, Barbra, John, Fi, Elizabeth, Josh, Dan, Ben, Nevada, Shawn, Garrick, Ryan, Zeb, Karen, Francesco, Steve, David, Sean, Gary, Jack, Jay, Adam, Jason, Tony, Derek, Andy, Dan, Kevin, Ben, Jess, Marcus, Travis, Mary, Simon, Gabino, Nathan, Benoit, Josh, Paul, Peter, Chris, Phil, Bethany, Nigel, Cat, Anthony, Rory, Ben, Kate, Guy, Lou, Jeramy, Carol, Andrew, Brett, Julian, Jason, Greg, Robb, Livius, Tim, Glenn, and anyone I likely missed (you *know* who you are!).

Mum, Dad, Yoko and Cocoa of course.

Hats off to Dominic at Roundfire – who gave me this invaluable shot in the dark, and has continually supported my 'artistic' judgment – along with Maria, Stuart, Nick, Trevor, Ben, John and Krystina.

Lastly? You, the reader of these very words. You rock my li'l world.

Andrez Bergen.
Tokyo, 2016

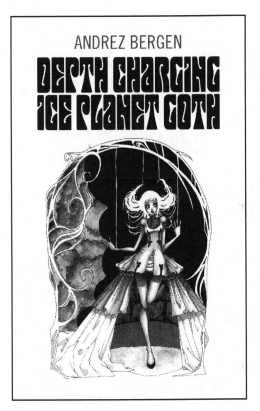

She's a disturbed, quiet girl, but Mina wants to do some good
out there. It's just that the world gets in the way. This is
Australia in the 1980s, a haven for goths and loners, where a
coming-of-age story can only veer into a murder mystery.

ISBN-13: 978-1782796497

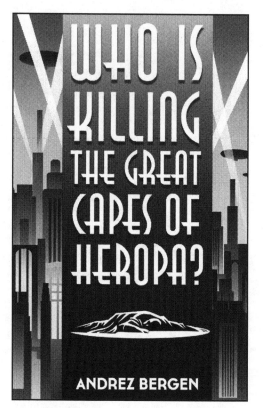

Heropa: A vast, homogenized city patrolled by heroes and
populated by adoring masses. A pulp-fiction fortress of solitude
for crime-fighting team the Equalizers, led by new recruit
Southern Cross — a lifetime away from the rain-drenched,
dystopic metropolis of Melbourne.
Who, then, is killing the great Capes of Heropa?
In this paired homage to detective noir from the 1940s and the
'60s Marvel age of trailblazing comic books, Andrez Bergen
gloriously redefines the mild-mannered superhero novel.

ISBN-13: 978-1782792352

AUTHOR PROFILE

Andrez Bergen is an expat Australian writer, journalist, DJ, artist and ad hoc saké connoisseur (from Melbourne) who's been entrenched in Tokyo, Japan, for the past 15 years. He lives with his wife and daughter.

Publications he's written for include *Mixmag*, *The Age*, *Australian Style*, *VICE*, and the *Yomiuri Shinbun*. Bergen has published six novels, wrote and illustrated three graphic novels, and published four comic book series – including *Bullet Gal*.

Bergen's fiction previously appeared through Crime Factory, Shotgun Honey, Snubnose Press, All Due Respect, Perfect Edge Books, Dirty Rotten Comics, Open Books, Roundfire Fiction, IF? Commix, Project-Nerd, and Another Sky Press, and he occasionally adapts scripts for feature films by the likes of Mamoru Oshii (*Ghost in the Shell*) for Production I.G in Japan.

Bergen also makes music as Little Nobody and Funk Gadget.

Roundfire

FICTION

Put simply, we publish great stories. Whether it's literary or
popular, a gentle tale or a pulsating thriller, the connecting
theme in all Roundfire fiction titles is that once you pick them
up you won't want to put them down.
If you have enjoyed this book, why not tell other readers by
posting a review on your preferred book site. Recent bestsellers
from Roundfire are:

The Bookseller's Sonnets
Andi Rosenthal
The Bookseller's Sonnets intertwines three love stories with a tale
of religious identity and mystery spanning five hundred years
and three countries.
Paperback: 978-1-84694-342-3 ebook: 978-184694-626-4

Birds of the Nile
An Egyptian Adventure
N.E. David
Ex-diplomat Michael Blake wanted a quiet birding trip up the
Nile – he wasn't expecting a revolution.
Paperback: 978-1-78279-158-4 ebook: 978-1-78279-157-7

Blood Profit$

The Lithium Conspiracy

J. Victor Tomaszek, James N. Patrick, Sr

The blood of the many for the profits of the few... *Blood Profit$*
will take you into the cigar-smoke-filled room where American
policy and laws are really made.

Paperback: 978-1-78279-483-7 ebook: 978-1-78279-277-2

The Burden

A Family Saga

N.E. David

Frank will do anything to keep his mother and father apart. But
he's carrying baggage - and it might just weigh him down...

Paperback: 978-1-78279-936-8 ebook: 978-1-78279-937-5

The Cause

Roderick Vincent

The second American Revolution will be a fire lit from an
internal spark.

Paperback: 978-1-78279-763-0 ebook: 978-1-78279-762-3

Don't Drink and Fly

The Story of Bernice O'Hanlon Part One

Cathie Devitt

Bernice is a witch living in Glasgow. She loses her way in her
life and wanders off the beaten track looking for the garden of
enlightenment.

Paperback: 978-1-78279-016-7 ebook: 978-1-78279-015-0

Gag
Melissa Unger
One rainy afternoon in a Brooklyn diner, Peter Howland
punctures an egg with his fork. Repulsed, Peter pushes the plate
away and never eats again.
Paperback: 978-1-78279-564-3 ebook: 978-1-78279-563-6

The Master Yeshua
he Undiscovered Gospel of Joseph
Joyce Luck
Jesus is not who you think he is. The year is 75 CE. Joseph ben
Jude is frail and ailing, but he has a prophecy to fulfil...
Paperback: 978-1-78279-974-0 ebook: 978-1-78279-975-7

On the Far Side, There's a Boy
Paula Coston
Martine Haslett, a thirty-something 1980s woman, plays hard on
the fringes of the London drag club scene until one night which
prompts her to sign up to a charity. She writes to a young Sri
Lankan boy, with consequences far and long.
Paperback: 978-1-78279-574-2 ebook: 978-1-78279-573-5

Tuareg
Alberto Vazquez-Figueroa
With over 5 million copies sold worldwide, *Tuareg* is a classic
adventure story from best-selling author Alberto Vazquez-
Figueroa, about honour, revenge and a clash of cultures.
Paperback: 978-1-84694-192-4

Readers of ebooks can buy or view any of these bestsellers by clicking on the live link in the title. Most titles are published in paperback and as an ebook.

Paperbacks are available in traditional bookshops. Both print and ebook formats are available online.

Find more titles and sign up to our readers' newsletter at http://www.johnhuntpublishing.com/fiction.

Follow us on Facebook at
https://www.facebook.com/JHPfiction
and Twitter at https://twitter.com/JHPFiction.